GRAVE HERITAGE

Copyright © 2016 by Blanche Day Manos

All rights reserved. No part of this book may be used or reproduced in any manner, including electronic storage and retrieval systems, except by explicit written permission from the publisher. Brief passages excerpted for review purposes are excepted.

This novel is a work of fiction. Names, characters, places, and incidents are either the product of the author's imagination or are used fictitiously. Though this is a work of fiction, many of the stories and anecdotes included were inspired by actual events. Some names used in this book are those of real people; however, any dialogue or activity presented is purely fictional.

ISBN: 978-1-68313-031-4

First Edition

Printed and bound in the USA

Cover and interior design by Kelsey Rice

GRAVE HERITAGE

A Darcy & Flora Cozy Mystery

Blanche Day Manos

P
Pen-L Publishing
Fayetteville, Arkansas
Pen-L.com

Books by Blanche Day Manos

~ The Darcy & Flora Mysteries ~
with Barbara Burgess:

The Cemetery Club
Grave Shift
Best Left Buried
Grave Heritage

~ The Ned McNeil Mysteries ~

Moonlight Can Be Murder

*Dedicated to Matt, Dawn, Sara and Nathan Manos
and to the memory of Bob and Susie Day*

Chapter 1

I awoke sitting straight up in bed, my heart doing double time. Was it rain pounding against my bedroom windows or the wind roaring around the house that had awakened me? Jethro, his feline apprehension alerted by my sudden movement, jumped off my bed and darted from the room.

Straining to hear, I hardly dared to breathe. There! It wasn't the wind; someone was banging on the front door.

Sliding my feet into house shoes, I trotted into the hall. Mom hurried from her room, a robe around her shoulders.

"Darcy," she whispered, gripping my arm. "What was that noise?"

"Someone is at the door." I don't know why we whispered; no one could have heard us above the clamor of the storm.

We crept downstairs, our way lit by continuously flashing lightning. Rain, flung against the house as if by a giant hand, sluiced down the windows. The frantic pounding came again.

"What poor soul would be out on a night like this?" Mom said, going to the door.

I grabbed her arm. "No, wait! Let me look first." Pulling aside the curtain, I craned my neck to see the porch. She was right. The drenched person who huddled there did indeed look like a poor soul. He was dripping and shivering, but with lightning flashes illuminating his hunched shape, he seemed more menacing than pitiful. What was he doing out here, far from town in such a downpour?

"I am going to get Dad's gun," I said. "Don't open the door until I tell you."

She frowned. "What? Why, Darcy?"

"Because there's a man on our porch in the middle of the night and we don't know who he is. Whether he needs help or not, we've got to be cautious. Who knows? He may be armed or dangerous."

Mom sniffed. "I guess."

At our former home in Levi, I had kept Dad's pistol in a drawer of the bookshelf. This new house also had a large, built-in bookshelf with drawers, most handy hiding places. Mom, ever trusting, would never have thought about the gun, but I, a seasoned investigative reporter for the Dallas Morning News and ever suspicious, felt safer knowing it was there.

My fingers touched the cold metal of that reassuring firearm. Holding it behind my back, I nodded toward Mom.

"Okay, switch on the porch light and open the door."

She swung the door inward and stepped back. A wet and bedraggled man stumbled into the living room. The first thing I thought of was a drowned rat, not that I had ever seen one. The man's thin, gray hair was plastered against his scalp. He was smallish, and being bent over seemed to be his normal stance. Rain dripped from his beak-like nose and ran down his stubbly chin.

Wiping his eyes, he blinked at us.

"Thanks," he croaked. "I was about to drown out there."

Fearful that Mom was going to offer him a towel to dry off and maybe invite him to the kitchen for a piece of pie, I tried to forestall the Southern hospitality for which she was famous.

Although a born Oklahoman, my first impulse was to be careful instead of hospitable. "Who are you?" I asked. "What are you doing out in the storm? Did your car break down somewhere?"

The man squinted at me, then his gaze shifted back to Mom. Again, he rubbed his hand across his eyes as he leaned forward and peered closely at her. He swallowed a couple of times, licked his lips, and asked in a hoarse whisper,

"Never mind who I am. Who are you?"

Sidling away from such close scrutiny, Mom said, "I'm Flora Tucker and this is my daughter, Darcy Campbell."

The man's face underwent a change. His mouth dropped open and his eyes widened. He backed out of the door, whirled around, and bolted across the porch, disappearing into the darkness.

Mom slammed the door, locked it, and drew a deep breath.

"Whew! What in the world was that about?" she asked. "Who was that strange little man and what scared him off? Did he see your gun, Darcy?"

"No. I kept it behind me. I don't think you look particularly scary, Mom, but he sure gave you the once over. He didn't panic until you told him your name."

She nodded. "He seemed sort of familiar but I can't place him at all. Well! I've never heard of such a thing."

"Me either." I shook my head and replaced Dad's revolver. "Is there any leftover coffee we could heat up? I don't think I can go back to sleep and my nerves need some steadying."

My mother raised her eyebrows. "Leftover coffee? I sure don't want my coffee to be secondhand. It won't take long to fix a new potful. I feel chilled through and through, and like you said, we won't be able to get back to sleep anyhow."

Mom was of the firm opinion that a cup of steaming Folgers coffee and prayer could fix just about anything. I agreed. Maybe if we thought about this night visitor long enough, we could come up with some reason for his appearance and abrupt departure. Or perhaps she would remember why he seemed familiar to her. Soon the cheerful sound of coffee perking in her old yellow coffee pot vied with the noise of the storm. She poured a couple of cups and we sat down at the table.

"This was such a peaceful day," I said, staring into my cup as if I could find answers there. "I love it out here on Granny Grace's old home site. I like the quiet of the country and I sure like this new house.

But, you know, I had a funny feeling all day that something wasn't quite right. Do you know what I mean?"

Mom nodded. "I do. I felt the same way but laid it onto the fact that a storm was coming. I was hoping that we were leaving all the mysterious stuff behind us in Levi and now, here's another mystery—a stranger on our front porch. I wonder why in the world, after knocking on the door, he turned around and ran."

"I'd say he wasn't expecting to see you, Mom. I think he really needed shelter from the storm but when he saw you, he recognized you and panicked. I don't know why mysteries follow us around. Maybe it's just me. After all, you led a pretty quiet life until I came back to Levi after Jake died."

Mom patted my hand. "I guess you're a mystery magnet, Darcy. My goodness, it kind of hurts my feelings that I look scarier than a thunderstorm. I keep thinking I should know him but for the life of me, I can't recall where I've seen him."

Laying the problem of our night visitor aside, Mom and I discussed her current project, building a school for homeless boys who needed a firm hand to keep them on the straight and narrow. *Ben's Boys* was to be the name of the school, named for its benefactor, Ben Ventris. After Mom's longtime friend passed away, she found that Ben had bequeathed all his worldly goods to her, including his farm. It was this farm that she, with the help of a good building contractor and Hiram Schuster, was turning into an attractive home and school for boys. Hiram, a lifelong friend, was music director at our church and a carpenter before he retired.

Two hours later as the ever-optimistic robins greeted the dawn of a new day, we still had no idea of the identity of our caller. Who was the night visitor, why had he banged on our door, and—most importantly—what made him run like a frightened rabbit back into the wind and rain?

Chapter 2

"That old setting hen is just going to have to take care of her eggs with no help from me," Mom said, coming into the kitchen through the back porch. Jethro padded along behind her.

Turning from the sink, I noticed she was rubbing her hand.

"Did she peck you?" I asked.

She nodded. "That's the last time I'm going to give her the chance, though. I was just trying to see if any eggs were broken. She didn't understand, I guess."

Laughing, I hung the dish cloth across the sink and wiped my wet hands on my jeans. Reaching under a hen whose mind was fixed on becoming a mother was not something I would want to do. The angry look in a chicken's yellow eyes and the sharpness of a hen's beak were enough to wilt any good intentions I might have.

"You have a beautiful new house with all the very latest in a lovely kitchen, but you had to have that flock of laying hens and a rooster in that pen out back," I teased.

And indeed this home was lovely. We had mulled over the builder's plans for so long that our new two-storied beauty with the wrap-around porch was exactly what we both wanted. Thanks to Dad's insurance policy, as well as my husband Jake's life insurance, money was not a problem at the moment, but it seemed odd not to have a job. I still freelanced for The Dallas Morning News but that did not require a lot of time. My mother would be a country woman, whether she was rich or poor. She loved the country life. And, to be honest, I felt the same.

I gazed out of the kitchen window at the sun-warmed herb garden, which meandered into the surrounding woods. The gray-green leaves of a mullein plant moved as a spotted leopard frog jumped under them. We tried to disturb nature as little as possible with our presence and just enjoyed the wild creatures that lived here with us.

The house sat on a knoll overlooking Lee Creek. A long driveway twisted between centuries-old trees and crossed a picturesque wooden bridge as it wound its way to a detached garage in back. The house had plenty of storage and two fireplaces, one in the downstairs guest room and one in the living room. It boasted a bright and well-equipped kitchen. Nestled among cottonwoods, oaks, and maples that grew in happy profusion throughout Ventris County, it was my idea of a dream come true.

After my husband Jake died, more than a year ago, I left Dallas and came back to my hometown of Levi, Oklahoma. I wanted peace and quiet and healing. Although I had seen very little of the peace and quiet, I kept hoping. The healing was slowly taking place, thanks in large part to Ventris County's tall, slim, red-haired sheriff, Grant Hendley. Grant had been my first sweetheart and, quite unexpectedly, those long-ago feelings were kindling back to life.

The sunny morning directly contrasted the stormy and strange night with the spooked stranger. My mother and I had stayed up after his visit because we were so wired we knew we couldn't relax enough to go back to sleep. Consequently, this morning my eyes felt heavy.

"I'm going into town and check on the house," I told her, heading for my purse and the keys to my Ford Escape. Our house in Levi where I grew up sat empty now that we had moved. I kept close tabs on it, though. It was a dear place to me because it had been my childhood home.

"I'll pick up some fruit juice to make the punch for our housewarming while I'm in town. Is there anything else we'll need?"

"Pat is bringing dozens of cookies," Mom answered. "It does seem like a lot of hoopla but several people have asked about our house. It seems almost like bragging to me, or showing off, but I'm happy for our friends to see where we live now so they can come and visit. I hope they feel as welcome here as they did at our old house."

"I'm sure they will," I said. "A housewarming is kind of like a welcome party for everyone. I hope it won't be raining. Although, you'll have to admit, a storm like the one we had last night might lend atmosphere."

Mom sighed. "I can do without that kind of atmosphere. I almost forgot to tell you that Pat called and said our new preacher is looking for a place to stay. She was wondering whether he'd want to rent our house in town."

"A new preacher, huh? Unless he has a big family, he really won't need a house as large as ours. But, I guess a preacher would be a good renter, quiet, no wild parties, hopefully pay his rent on time."

Leaning against the counter, Mom grinned at me. "Well, for goodness sake, let's hope." The small church we attended looked like it was straight from a Norman Rockwell print. It was made of wood, painted white, had a belfry and, believe it or not, a bell that rang each Sunday morning calling the faithful to worship. The pastor, a dear elderly man, had recently retired and left on an extended vacation to Florida. Our congregation was limping along with lay preachers until we could find a new shepherd for the flock.

"Wait!" Mom stopped me as I was going out of the door. "Will you check in with the Jenkins sisters? They have some herbs they want to give me to add to the ones I've already planted." She chuckled. "Miss Georgia is determined that I should make my own herbal tea."

"Sure," I said. Our new relationship with the Jenkins twins was one of the most surprising things about the last few months. Even though our closeness with these two ladies had deepened, we still referred to them as we always had—Miss Georgia and Miss Carolina.

Lee Creek gurgled under our wood bridge with a lot more enthusiasm than before last night's storm. Driving into Levi, I noticed several branches off the trees but no real damage that I could see. The fragrance of green, growing vegetation wafted into my car. Summer's heat had not yet laid an oppressive hand over Ventris County and the world looked newly-washed and bursting with the energy of July.

After I checked our empty house and got the herbs from Miss Georgia, I planned to have lunch with Grant. My heart quickened, thinking about Levi's handsome sheriff. I could hardly wait to see him, although it was only a couple of days ago that he had been to our house for supper.

A movement caught my eye as I neared Old String Road. Glancing in the direction of the tumbledown house that had belonged to Old String, our local recluse and hoarder, I saw smoke curling up over the treetops. I braked and peered through a tangle of vines and tree branches. My breath caught in my throat. Flames flickered along the sagging roof. The shack was on fire.

Swinging off the main road, I sped to the ramshackle building and stopped a few yards away. I jumped from my car and trotted nearer. What had started this inferno? Had lightning struck it during the storm and had it smoldered all night? It had been vacant since Old String died and would be no great loss. Surely the trees and grass were wet enough to keep the fire from spreading. Still, perhaps I should call the fire department.

As I walked closer, I made out a smoking roof. Yes, I had better call 911 and ask for the fire truck. Those low-hanging tree branches could possibly begin to blaze.

Coughing, I swatted at the thick smoke stinging my eyes and throat. I did not see the body lying on the ground in the tall grass until I stumbled over it. My heart hammered into my throat as I dropped to my knees beside the crumpled figure of a man. Lifting his bony hand, I felt for a pulse. Nothing. Life no longer beat within this human form. A ragged, reddish-brown splotch stained his shirt front. I got slowly to my feet, staring down at the pale face, stubbly beard and beak-like nose. I had seen this man once before, only a few hours ago.

Chapter 3

Twenty minutes later, I sat in Grant's truck, clutching a cup of coffee from his thermos, Old String's house a charred tumble of boards and shingles in front of us. Only two partial walls stood with a section of roof slanting down over them, accidentally forming a small remnant of a room. These remains looked as if they could collapse with the next gust of wind. The firemen replaced their equipment and prepared to go back to Levi. An ambulance had already taken away that pitiful figure I had found in the yard.

Grant put his arm around my shoulders. "You're shaking so much you're going to spill your coffee."

Taking a deep breath, I gulped the steaming brew and nodded. My teeth chattered as if I had a chill. Nothing at the moment could ease the image of that lifeless body lying on the ground.

"That poor devil on the ground—I've never seen him around town. He may have been a vagrant—a homeless person who took shelter in the shack last night," Grant muttered, watching the fire truck turn around. "But who killed him? And why? I'm guessing whoever did it tried to burn down the house with the guy inside, but if that's the case, he stumbled out before he went up in flames. Or, maybe it was lightning."

"Um, Grant, he may have been a vagrant, but I'm pretty sure I've seen him. I'm not certain; he looks so different, um, dead, but I think he's the person who came to our door last night during the storm."

Grant frowned. "He came to your house?"

I downed more coffee. "Someone knocked on our door while the storm was at its worst. When Mom let him in, he took a good look at her then bolted back into the rain. It was like he recognized my mother. She thought he looked familiar too but couldn't figure out why."

Swallowing the last drop and replacing the plastic cup over the thermos, I turned toward Grant. "Are you sure he was murdered? Maybe he fell on something. Could it have been an accidental death?"

Even as I asked, I feared the answer.

I had the feeling Grant's thoughts were far from the fire truck as he gazed at its slow trek down the road toward Levi.

"I'll have Doc McCauley give me his verdict," he said, "but I think he was murdered, Darcy. That man did not die of a heart attack. He wasn't burned in the fire. I didn't see anything he might have fallen on; besides, he was lying on his back. That wound wasn't a gunshot but, from the look of things, I'd say the murder weapon was something sharp, something at close range."

Shutting my eyes, I tried to swallow the sick feeling that rose in my throat, seeing again the bloody shirt and the man's staring eyes and gaping mouth. Who would hate another person enough to do that to him?

A sharp rap on the side of the truck jarred my eyes open.

Grant's deputy, Jim Clendon, poked his arm through the window. "Say, I just found this near the house. The firemen stepped on it and smashed it into the mud, but it don't look like it's been there long."

He handed a knife to Grant. It was a pocket knife, a common variety except for one thing: lettering on the side that proclaimed it to be a promotional item from a local builder. My breath caught in my throat. I had seen a knife similar to that not too long ago. Pat Harris's son Jasper had one like it. For that matter, so did I but mine was still in the gun drawer at home. Jasper's was unique in that some of the letters on the side of his knife were missing. The visible ones, C, H, m, s recently helped guide us to a killer. These same letters were on the handle of the knife Jim found.

Grant's face hardened. I knew that he remembered Jasper's knife too. Jasper was a loner, a young man who liked to roam through the woods. He would never harm anyone—I was sure of it—but he was different, a little odd, and lots of people did not understand that. In addition, Jasper had the unhappy tendency to be in the wrong place at the wrong time. When Ben Ventris was killed, Grant had suspected Jasper at first. And then Andrea Worth's disappearance; Jasper had known a lot about that.

Grant's voice was grim. "Are you able to drive, Darcy? If not, I'll run you home and Jim can follow."

"I can drive," I said. My voice sounded shaky to my own ears. "I need to tell Mom about this before she hears it on the news."

"Or from Pat Harris?" Grant asked quietly.

I nodded. "Or from Pat."

Chapter 4

Mom kept shaking her head. We sat at her old wood dining table, mugs of coffee close at hand. Jethro, who sensed when I needed a furry head to stroke, left his food dish, strolled over to the table and sprang onto my lap.

"I don't understand it," Mom said. "Just think, only a little while after he was here, that fellow was murdered. It gives me the chills."

"Me too, Mom."

"And Jim found Jasper's knife at the old house?"

"Well, it looks like Jasper's. I'm sure there are lots of knives around town that look like his. We have one too. Only thing is, the knife Jim found has the same lettering as Jasper's."

Mom swallowed a sip of coffee. "I haven't even seen that knife of ours for months. I don't like knives or guns. Rightfully, I guess our knife belongs to Jackson Conner. It was his to start with."

I nodded. "I don't think he wants it. Maybe you would feel better if you gave Jackson a call."

"And tell him what?" Mom asked.

"I just thought maybe he could say some comforting words."

Smiling, Mom said, "Darcy, I'm not that delicate. Now, I enjoy talking to Jackson, but he's busy and I don't want to bother him unless we find out we need him, maybe for Jasper, if he actually becomes an official suspect."

Jackson Conner, Levi's most popular lawyer, was also my mother's dear friend. Or maybe a little more than a friend? I certainly could see the attraction. Jackson had white hair and a bushy mustache, keen, blue eyes, and was altogether the most comforting man I knew. He was also my mother's ardent admirer.

And Mom? Well, I could only hope I looked as good as she when I was closing in on seven decades on this earth. From her Cherokee ancestors she had inherited dark hair, high cheekbones and beautiful tan skin. She moved with grace and dignity and glowed with good health. She could work circles around me any day without tiring.

Thankfully, I shared many of her physical characteristics, the facial structure and skin color. Although my hair was dark too, I wore it long. The only thing I had inherited from my Irish dad, Andy Tucker, was his peppery temper.

The clack of tires bumping over our wooden bridge interrupted my thoughts. Looking out the window, I saw Patricia Harris's truck pull to a stop in the driveway.

Drawing a long breath, I glanced at Mom.

"Oh, boy! Here comes Pat now. I wonder if she has heard about the dead man?"

"I'm not going to mention him, if she hasn't," Mom called over her shoulder, hurrying to open the door.

From the tenor of Pat's voice, I judged that she was upset.

Mom tried to calm her as she guided Pat into the dining room.

Jethro sprang off my lap and dashed toward the comparative quiet of the living room.

"Now, Pat, just sit down at the table and I'll pour you a cup of coffee. I can't make head nor tail of what you are saying," Mom said as she went toward the coffee pot.

Pat's face under her tight, gray curls was as red as the rose in our yard in Levi. She was puffing sort of like a steam engine as she plopped down in a chair and grabbed the mug of coffee Mom handed her.

"I tell you, Flora, that Grant Hendley has some nerve, to come to my house and demand to see Jasper. Said something about just wanting to know where Jasper was last night during the storm and wanted to talk to him this morning. Why, even I don't know where Jasper is half the time and anyway, doesn't he have a right to roam the woods if he wants to? Grant wouldn't tell me the reason he wanted to talk to Jasper, but why is it my boy is the first one who comes to his mind every time something happens? What I want you to tell me, Flora Tucker, is what's going on. If anybody knows, I figure it's you or Darcy, because you always seem to be right smack in the middle of trouble."

"You'll feel better if you drink your coffee," Mom suggested as Pat ran out of air.

Pat swallowed a mouthful of coffee, choked and gasped, and then, with visible effort, took some deep breaths.

Reaching across the table, I squeezed her hand. "Now, Miss Pat, don't be upset. You see, that shack of Old String's burned down this morning—"

Pat interrupted, eyes bulging. "It did?"

I nodded. "It did and, you see, I found a dead man in the yard, and—"

"A dead man? Darcy Campbell, I might have known! Why is it that people just sort of wait until you get there before they decide to turn up their toes and go meet their Maker? I didn't notice anything unusual about you when you were a little girl, although you always had more than a healthy dose of curiosity but…who was the dead man?"

Before she could deliver another rant, Mom spoke up. "We don't know yet who he was, but just think a minute. When somebody is murdered—"

"Murdered?" Pat squawked. "Oh, my great aunt's garters! And Grant suspects my poor Jasper."

Shaking my head, I said, "No, no, he doesn't, Miss Pat. He just has to check out everybody. Maybe he wants to talk to Jasper because Jasper sometimes knows things that other people don't."

Slowly, Pat nodded. "Well now, I hadn't thought of that. Yes, maybe that's it. Jasper does seem to know what's going on in these woods. Grant talking to him about that would be fine, but the truth is I don't know where Jasper is. I haven't seen him since supper last night. How awful that there has been another murder in Ventris County. Who in the world would have been out there at Old String's shack anyway? Maybe a homeless person although—"

I interrupted, which was sometimes the only way to carry on a conversation with Pat. Changing the subject seemed like a good idea.

"You said the new preacher might be interested in renting our house?"

"Yes, that's right." Pat's voice dropped an octave or two as her face slowly returned to its normal color. "As a member of the pulpit committee, it's my job to look around for a place for him to stay. He's from somewhere down south so he'll be a long way from home. Your house is pretty big for one person, but he might like it anyway. It's kind of on the edge of town, quiet, and there's that pasture behind the house."

Mom got up to refill our coffee cups. "He isn't married, then? I thought the church preferred a married man, thinking he would be more stable."

I laughed. "Nobody at this table is married and I think we are about as stable as they come."

"I meant to call you, Flora, and tell you that the preacher would like to go look at the house today, this morning in fact, but in all the excitement with Grant's visit, I forgot."

"I was on my way to town when I saw that house burning," I said, glancing at the clock. "It's nearly noon and I've got some stops to make in Levi, so I'd better be on my way. I'm looking forward to meeting this mysterious minister. Maybe he'll drop in while I'm at the house. If he's elderly, the stairs might be a problem."

"I don't think he's old," Pat said. "His picture on the resume was not very good. He said he needed a quiet area because he's writing a book."

"Writing? Then we have something in common." Sometimes I doubted I would ever complete my second book about the stories and folklore of Ventris County. After I had finished the first book, I started this one but progress was mighty slow. My friend Amy kept prodding me to finish it, as did Mom. I had good intentions but I knew what road good intentions paved.

Shaking my head, I went out to the garage. Preachers were hard to come by. The church had been searching for a couple of months and was probably glad for any candidate, young, elderly, or in between. I imagined a quiet person, a devout man of God, just the type of renter we were looking for.

Chapter 5

The tangy scents of rosemary and peppermint perfumed the car. Drawing a deep breath of the heavenly fragrances that came from the herbs nestling in the Escape's cargo area, I thought about my visit with the Jenkins twins. Visiting with Miss Georgia and Miss Carolina usually left me with a contented glow.

Their warm hugs as they had invited me into their huge, shady house with the wide and high front porch made me grateful for these two ladies in my life.

"Now, keep that mint in a pot, Darcy, honey," Miss Georgia had said. "Mint just goes wild if you put it in the ground with nothing around it to make it behave."

"There's all kinds of mint," Miss Carolina added. "I kind of like for it to run free; doesn't bother me if it takes over. There's pineapple mint and chocolate mint. Even out in the woods, there's horse mint. I remember walking through it as a girl and smelling good the rest of the day."

After a cup of tea (herbal, of course) and instructions on the care of an herb garden, I said goodbye to the Jenkins twins and headed for Mom's house.

Mom had decided to keep, rather than sell, the beautiful old home I had grown up in. Earthquakes had damaged it somewhat last year, but we'd had it repaired and inspected to be sure it was safe. I didn't think I could bear for anybody else to own it with its memories of Dad and Grant and even Jake on our visits home from Dallas. When Mom and I moved into the new house, we took her dining table, her yellow coffee pot, and several pieces of furniture but left the rest. Placed among the new sofa and chairs, beds, and appliances, the familiar pieces made our present home seem more comfortable.

To have started in such a horrific manner with the fire and dead body, this day was turning out to have some bright spots. Grant had phoned before I reached the Jenkinses' home. The result was he would pick me up at the old house and we would go for that delayed lunch.

As I parked in the familiar driveway and climbed out of my SUV, a roar behind me stopped me in my tracks. Coming toward me was a big, black motorcycle ridden by someone wearing a helmet and goggles. As I watched, the cyclist pulled into the driveway, cruised past my car and mowed a path through my mother's bed of zinnias.

"Hey! Are you blind?" I yelled.

Pushing the kickstand down with a black-booted foot, the stranger swung off his cycle's deep leather seat and faced me. When he pulled off his helmet and goggles, I did a double-take. This man was tall, almost as tall as Grant. His hair was dark and curly. His eyes were midnight blue, fringed with long lashes. He was beyond attractive; he was movie-star handsome and he reminded me of Jake.

"I'm sorry, Ma'am," he said with a Southern drawl. "I was so taken with the beauty of this house that I didn't look where I was going. I'll certainly pay for those lovely flowers, if you'll tell me what I owe you."

I gulped and shook my head. "Money can't replace that flower garden. Just pay attention next time, please. Why are you here? Were you following me?"

Perfect white teeth glinted as he laughed. "Following? No, I wasn't following. I heard this house might be for rent and I was hoping to meet with the owner. Would that be you?"

What was there about this stranger that reminded me of my husband? His dark hair? The light in his eyes? Or, maybe it was just the energy I felt emanating from him. He made me uncomfortable.

"It would," I snapped, "but I think it's already spoken for. Our new preacher is supposed to look at it."

With a disarming grin which showed a deep dimple in his cheek, he said, "That would be me, Trace Hughes, Miss…"

A preacher? A Clark Gable look-alike on a motorcycle? I think I meant to shake hands with him. Maybe I was just going to lean against the motorcycle for support, which was a foolish idea, but shock froze my brain. However it happened, I stepped toward Trace Hughes, stumbled, and my capri-encased leg grazed the exhaust pipe of his cycle. It was hot!

"Ow!" I yelled, dropping to the ground and grabbing my leg. The spot which had come in contact with the motorcycle was red and quickly forming a blister. It hurt, not just a little, but a lot.

The preacher knelt beside me. Gently, he turned my leg toward him and scrutinized the burn.

"I'm so sorry again," he said, his eyes meeting mine. "This sure isn't the way I planned to introduce myself to the town of Levi. I think we'd better get you to a doctor."

"Could I be of assistance?" asked a familiar but strangely cold voice.

Glancing up, I saw Grant glaring down at us. His thumbs were hooked in his belt, his hat was tilted over his eyes and, if the unsmiling line of his mouth was any indication, I guessed that he was not the least bit happy.

Chapter 6

"Wear short pants for a while, keep this ointment on it, and change the bandage every day," Doc McCauley said.

I slid from his examining table and took a few steps toward the door.

"Thanks, Doc," I mumbled. "I don't know what you put in that shot but it's good stuff. My leg doesn't hurt at all now. In fact, I've never felt better."

The doctor laughed and stopped me with a hand on my shoulder.

"The door is in the other direction, Darcy," he said.

Grant rose from his chair and took my arm. "I'll get her home, Doc," he said.

"Yes," I muttered, blinking as the doctor's face swam into focus. "Thank goodness, Grant can drive me home."

A few minutes later, Grant and I were on the road. I closed my eyes, engulfed in a pleasant haze of drowsiness and well-being.

"So, the man who made such a burning impression is your new pastor?" Grant asked.

"Hmm? Who? Oh, yes. His name is Trace Hughes. Cute, isn't he?"

In my right mind, I never would have said anything like that to Grant, but my mind was wrapped in the cozy comfort of painlessness and was definitely muddled.

Silence met my comment.

It was a quiet ride home. I wished I could bottle that warm feeling of contentment, of being safe and cared for. In fact, I think I may have dozed.

The rattle of planks beneath the tires of my SUV as Grant drove over our bridge woke me. I roused, stretched, and smiled at my chauffeur.

"Thanks so much, Grant. I certainly was in no condition to drive. You were a lifesaver."

"Just stay away from the exhaust pipe of motorcycles in the future, Darcy. I don't know how all that happened and I don't think I want to know," he said.

After my nap, I felt surprisingly refreshed and my thinking skills were returning. There was something important I needed to ask Grant. Oh, yes! The dead man's identity.

"I should have thought of this before we left the doctor's office, but I forgot, thanks to that wonderful med. Does Dr. McCauley plan to do an autopsy on the person I found by Old String's shack? Does he know the man's name?" I asked.

A grin tugged at Grant's mouth. "Little Miss Curiosity. The doctor wouldn't have told you, Darcy, and neither will I. This is an ongoing police investigation. Don't start meddling and trying to find out who the guy was or who did him in. Just let us handle it, okay?"

Well, rats! Did he say "meddling"? *Anybody* would be curious. After all, the man had come to our house and then dashed back into the storm and to his death. Didn't that give me a right to be let in on a few investigative secrets?

I unhooked my seat belt. "All right, Grant."

That wasn't really a promise, was it? What I meant was I would consider his advice and I certainly didn't plan on placing my mother in danger. Or me, for that matter. But how in the world was I not supposed to think about this bizarre murder and the way it seemed to implicate Jasper Harris?

A white Ford truck pulled in behind us.

"There's Jim to take me back to town," Grant said. "I'll carry those flowers in for you. They sure smell strong, don't they?"

"Those plants aren't really flowers," I said. "They're herbs from Miss Georgia. An herb is sort of a weed—a weed with an attitude."

He leaned toward me and gave me a swift peck on my cheek. "Just get well and stay safe. And stay out of trouble."

"Yes, Sir," I muttered. To my credit, I didn't salute. But I felt like it. The only complaint I had about Grant was his bossiness. I had known him since we were kids. He was bossy then and he was still bossy.

Chapter 7

"There!" I said, rising to my feet with the help of a hoe handle. My burned leg felt stiff and made kneeling a challenge. "That was the last sweet basil to go in the ground. We've done a good morning's work, Mom."

My mother straightened a stepping stone and stood up, her hand on her back. "It's so aggravating when I can't get down on my knees without my joints complaining. Getting old, I guess."

I laughed. "That'll be the day. You're as young as springtime! You have planted more herbs this morning than I have. I really like the way you're arranging this area, with the paving stones going through the whole garden, and the bench by the bird bath."

We stood admiring our handiwork. Miss Georgia's herbs joined those that we planted earlier. Mom had plotted out the whole garden last winter before we moved, determined to keep a natural, woodsy look. She had succeeded! A few dogwood trees grew among the herbs and even a couple of sumac bushes.

She'd defended her choice when I questioned leaving the lowly sumac where we found it, growing among the dogwoods.

"Those leaves turn a beautiful color in the fall," she said. "I don't want to disturb these woods any more than necessary. The trees were here before anybody thought about building a house and I want to keep them. I'll just plant my herb garden in places that won't bother anything that's already growing."

She even brought the old mossy rock from the house in town that had been in my grandparents' barnyard many years ago, just to add to the natural look. It was as if the rock had never left the farm.

Taller herbs like the bee balm and lavender grew among rosemary and sage. Garlic also found a home in the herb garden. Along and between the stepping stones, Mom had planted creeping phlox and lemon thyme.

"Walking through your garden is indulging in aromatherapy," I told her. "It's beautiful and it smells heavenly."

She pushed a strand of hair back from her face and smiled. "Yes, I love it out here. Maybe next year we can set up a small pond with a stream. Someday it'll be as pretty as Miss Georgia's."

Putting my arm around her, I said. "I think it is prettier right now. I like it!"

"The Jenkinses' garden is a lot older, though. It probably has been by their back door for nearly a hundred years, or at least since the older Jenkinses lived there. I imagine herbs were pretty important to serving a tasty meal in the old days." She broke off a spearmint leaf and popped it into her mouth. "And for home remedies."

In truth, we had taken several ideas, in addition to the herbs, from the Jenkins home. Our garage, for instance, which we placed behind our house, was modeled after an old-fashioned carriage house. So was the Jenkinses' garage. The only difference was we had an automatic door opener and they didn't. Stairs inside the garage led up to what was once living quarters for servants at the Jenkinses' home, while our garage upstairs space was empty just now except for a few boxes and odds and ends left over from when we moved.

My cell phone beeped. I glanced at it and saw a familiar number.

"Thoughts must be powerful," I said. "It looks like Miss Georgia or Miss Carolina is calling right now."

Punching the "talk" button, I said hello.

"Darcy?" came the quavery voice of Miss Georgia. "Darcy, honey, do you believe in ghosts?"

"What is it?" Mom asked, as I stood there with my mouth open. "Is someone sick?"

Covering the mouthpiece, I said, "I don't know. Miss Georgia just asked me if I believe in ghosts."

Mom caught her breath. "Tell her I'm on my way," she said.

Chapter 8

"I'm beginning to think my sister and I are ready for the old folks' home," Miss Carolina said, bringing a tray laden with four cups and saucers, a teapot and a small silver flask into the Jenkins living room. "I baked an apple pie this morning and set it on the cabinet to cool. After that, Georgia and I walked over to the church to see if Gladys Holcutt needed any help readying the church for Sunday. She's not getting any younger, you know, and running the sweeper over the carpet is a big job for one person. When we came back home, that pie had vanished!"

I took a drink of tea to hide my smile and shook my head when Miss Carolina waved the flask in my direction. She added a few drops of sherry to her herbal tea and to Miss Georgia's. A vanishing pie was the big mystery? Since it was impossible for something to disappear into thin air, maybe Miss Carolina had forgotten where she put it.

These two ladies poured their lives into the Methodist Church in Levi and I was sure their real reason for going to the church today was to be certain it had been cleaned to their satisfaction. The thought of the three elderly women—Miss Georgia, Miss Carolina and Miss Gladys—spiffying up the Methodist sanctuary struck me as funny. I could imagine them rising from their death beds to clean that church simply because nobody else would do it right.

So far as I knew, these three women were among Levi's oldest citizens. Their memories of the town's early days were priceless. Somehow,

I needed to find time to talk with them about some of those memories. They would be a wonderful addition to the book I was writing.

Miss Kitty, the beautiful and very old white Persian cat that belonged to these maiden ladies, floated into the room. I say floated because she moved as softly as a shadow and, with her long, white fur, reminded me of an unearthly spirit. Miss Kitty could not hear and neither did she speak. She opened her mouth and looked as if she were meowing but never made a sound. I loved that cat!

Gently, I lifted her to the sofa beside me.

"Miss Kitty," I said, playfully shaking my finger at her nose, "did you eat a whole pie all by yourself?"

Miss Georgia smiled and shook her head.

"By the way, did you rent your house here in town to your new preacher?" Miss Carolina asked.

Mom nodded. "Yes, he's all moved in and ready for church services Sunday."

It would have been nice if Miss Georgia and Miss Carolina attended church with us but our home church had always been Baptist.

Miss Georgia shook her head. "I think we're getting off the track here. What my sister is trying to say, and taking a mighty long time to say it, is that when we came back home from visiting with Gladys at the church, that pie was gone slick as a whistle and we can't find it anywhere."

Miss Carolina's eyes grew round and she spoke in a loud whisper. "In place of the pie was a dollar bill. Somebody had left a dollar on the cabinet."

Mom shook her head. "And I don't suppose you locked your doors as you left the house?"

"Why, of course not," Miss Carolina said. "We've never done that. Nobody dares come into the judge's house uninvited."

"Until now," I said, stroking Miss Kitty, who snuggled against my hand. The way these two women, who must have been nearing ninety, talked about their father as if the grouchy old man still lived with them, was irritating. I doubted that many people in Levi remembered the stern judge who meted out his idea of unbending justice, and they wouldn't fear his ghost if they did remember.

"You can't keep out spirits, Darcy, honey," Miss Georgia said, her forehead creased with worry. "Of course, we're used to the occasional whiff of tobacco smoke or the sound of a door closing, but we figure that's just Papa. He sort of inhabits the house now and then, you know. But Papa would never steal a pie. This may be an actual ghost."

"I can't imagine what sort of ghost would steal a pie and then leave a dollar," Miss Carolina interrupted.

I grinned. "A hungry but honest one?" Mom frowned at me.

Miss Georgia continued. "Last night when it was raining, I got out of bed because the lightning and thunder woke me. I glanced out the window and I saw something white flit through our herb bed. In the rain! Now, Carolina, don't look at me like that. I know I saw it."

"Well, that sure wasn't the judge," I muttered. "And it wouldn't have been Miss Kitty. She has never been out of the house."

"Never," Miss Georgia agreed.

If Judge Jenkins still came around to check on his spinster daughters and make sure they were behaving, he wouldn't swipe an apple pie. Not the austere old stickler for the law I had heard about. And he wouldn't have been flitting through the yard dressed in white. If he were a ghost, he'd be more the slamming-doors-and-stomping-down-hallways kind.

"Have there been other unexplained happenings besides the pie and the ghostly figure?" Mom asked.

"A couple of days ago, I put Delsie back into the garage and closed the door tight like I always do. A few minutes later I looked out and that door was open, swinging on its hinges, making the most awful squeaking sound." Miss Georgia shuddered and added a few more drops from the flask to her cup.

"You really should lock that garage as well as your house," I said. "That old car of your father's is a valuable antique and there are lots of people who'd like to own it or sell it."

Neither sister drove. Stores were within walking distance for them, but every so often they would back their father's 1940 black Chevrolet out of the garage and wipe it down. My mouth watered just thinking about it. If I should be so lucky as to inherit it someday, I would probably be just as particular with Delsie as were the twins.

Miss Carolina's eyes opened wide. "You're right, Darcy. Always so sensible. Maybe we should put a padlock on that door."

The roar of a small engine cut into our conversation. Looking out, I saw a man pushing a lawn mower around the house.

"I thought Burke Hopkins was mowing your grass," I said. "That doesn't look like Burke."

"Burke is kind of getting up in years and we've had so much rain this summer, the grass has grown like everything. We need to have it cut often and I think all that mowing was too much for Burke. He's busy with his own yard and that dog and those chickens of his," Miss Georgia said. "This man is Tim Johnson. He's new in town and said he needed to work."

Miss Carolina nodded. "He does a good job. Maybe you should talk to him about mowing your yard, Darcy. It's such a wilderness out there that it's really too hard for you to mow."

"I'll try to catch him before we leave," I agreed. "Now let's go look the place over and see if we can find a sign of an intruder," I said. "I don't believe in ghosts, Miss Georgia, but I'd prefer a spirit to a real, live person who is lurking around."

Moving slowly, so as not to disturb Miss Kitty, I got up and set my cup on the tray.

We looked all over the rambling old house, upstairs, downstairs, and in the attic.

"Be careful of that loose hand rail," Miss Georgia said as we went out the front door.

Going across the wide porch and down the steep front steps, we walked around the house, trying to peer in clouded basement windows until we got to the back yard.

"I've never been in your basement," I said. "Should we take a look in there?"

"Goodness, no," Miss Carolina said. "There's only one way in and that's by the kitchen pantry. We locked that door years ago. Nobody could get down there from out in the yard unless they went through a window or the coal chute. Why, Georgia and I haven't been down there for an age."

We looked at the herb bed but if there had been footprints, the rain had washed them away. Going into the garage, I made sure Delsie was all right and I even climbed to the garage loft. Sticking my head into that small room, I took a look around.

"I see absolutely nothing alarming," I told the three women who watched me with anxious eyes. "I have no idea what you saw but maybe it was a one-time occurrence, some vagrant passing through who was hungry. And honest."

They sighed in unison. "Well, if you say so, Darcy," Miss Carolina said.

Mom turned back to the house. "I think you've had enough excitement for one day. We'll let you know if anything unusual is happening anywhere else in town. Maybe there have been other break-ins. However, a pie is kind of an odd thing to steal, seems to me."

Mom and I were both quiet as we climbed into my car and started back home. What could be happening at the Jenkins house? Surely they were not both getting senile at the same time.

Shaking her head, Mom said, "You know, that's a mighty big old house for two defenseless and frail ladies to try and take care of. I wish they would come and live with us but I know they won't."

I snapped my fingers. "I forgot to talk to their lawn person. I'll ask Miss Georgia to tell him to call me. She's right. Our yard is kind of a challenge to mow."

I dodged a small limb in the road. "Maybe they just have a case of nerves. Miss Georgia probably imagined she saw somebody in the herb garden. And she may have thought she locked the garage door, but didn't."

"And what about the pie?" Mom asked. "Did it disappear by itself?"

I shrugged. "Sad to say, Miss Carolina could have put it someplace besides the cabinet top and forgot where she put it."

"Did she forget she put the dollar bill in its place? Somehow, Darcy, I don't think they are that forgetful. I'd like for it to be just their imagination, but I think there's more to it."

As it turned out, there was a whole lot more to it.

Chapter 9

I awoke Sunday morning with a feeling of anticipation. This was to be the first day for our new preacher, Trace Hughes, to fill the pulpit. I could hardly wait to hear him. And, to add to that excitement, our housewarming was scheduled for four o'clock that afternoon, giving people time to rest after church. The housewarming would also serve as sort of a get-acquainted party for our new minister.

The day promised to be beautiful and sunny, with only a few lumpy thunderheads along the horizon, a common sight during the summer months. This was a perfect day for worshiping the Lord then getting together with our friends and neighbors later.

Mom had wanted to have a sit-down country supper with brown beans, fried potatoes, cornbread and peach cobbler but I had talked her into keeping it simple. Just cookies and tea would do fine for a housewarming, I assured her.

The only extra activity was a brainchild of my friend Amy Miller. She wanted to introduce everyone not only to the house but to the surrounding countryside. She came up with the idea for a sunset stroll.

"Darcy," she said, "everybody is going to be interested in your mother's herb garden, Lee Creek, the old orchard and that deserted cemetery. Why don't we have a ghost walk?"

I bit my tongue to keep from yelling, "Are you crazy?" Instead, I exhibited amazing self-control, and my voice rose only a little when I said, "I don't want anybody to think our home is spooky. It's a wonderful, warm place. Sure, we can walk around outside and see what there is to see, but I'm not going to say anything about ghosts, for goodness sake!"

Amy, who was never one to give up easily, answered that at least we could wait until nearly dark, provide everyone with a flashlight and a map with places of interest marked on it, and the darkness would lend some atmosphere. I finally agreed. I didn't want the inclusion of a sunset stroll to take away from the warm, friendly get-together atmosphere.

Mom was just as eager to hear the new preacher as I. She was ready to go to church with time to spare. To me, my mother was always an attractive woman, but today she had taken special care, actually wearing a smidgen of lipstick. Her dark hair framed her face, and the lavender dress she chose to wear set off her olive skin.

I had heeded Dr. McCauley's advice about wearing pants that would not rub the burn on my leg, but I hesitated to wear capris to church. Yes, churches were much less formal than years past, and I liked the idea that we went to worship, not to show off our clothes; however, First Baptist of Levi, Oklahoma, had an old-fashioned congregation. We sang from hymnals, all the good old songs of the church; the women wore dresses, and the men wore long pants, mostly blue jeans.

So, I chose a full, blue, swirly skirt that came past the bandage on my leg, paired with a solid blue over blouse. I stuck my feet into a pair of black flats, piled my hair on top of my head, added lipstick and blusher and I was ready. In record time.

Pat Harris was our pianist. Each Sunday, she played a soothing prelude while people found their favorite pews, then the piano accompanied us as we sang. We may have been a bit off-key at times, but our hearts were in tune even if our voices were not.

Hiram Schuster had been our song leader since I could remember. He was not as robust as he once had been, and his voice sometimes quavered, but he waved his right arm vigorously, his left hand holding the song book, and sang lustily, a beatific smile on his wrinkled face.

The church parking lot was full of cars when we arrived and, as Mom and I entered the sanctuary, we felt lucky to see two empty spaces in our pew, second from the front, right side of the building. To my surprise, Grant was already seated there. Usually, he worked Sundays. He was not a regular churchgoer, although he was a Christian.

Pat was not at her usual place at the piano. Was she sick? And where was Trace Hughes?

The crowd stirred restlessly, probably wondering the same things Mom and I whispered about. Then, a hush descended as our minister walked up the aisle and stood in front of the podium.

I gasped. He wore faded blue jeans, a short-sleeved shirt which hung over his jeans, and brown cowboy boots, and he had a guitar slung over his shoulder.

"Good morning, dear flock," he drawled, grinning the wide smile that showed off his dimples. "We may do things a little differently this morning, but that's all right, isn't it? I don't believe the Lord always stuck to protocol, did He? I've asked Miss Pat and Hiram to take a well-deserved break this morning and I'm going to lead you in a few songs."

I glanced across the aisle at Hiram Schuster and his wife. Pat sat stiffly beside them, frowning, and none of the three looked like they were truly in the Spirit.

Trace propped his foot on the front pew, ran his fingers over the guitar, and a lovely arpeggio filled the sanctuary. Smiling, he belted out the first notes to "Great Is the Lord."

I sat up straight and my mouth dropped open. People turned toward each other and then back to the man at the front of the room. No professional guitarist or vocalist could have out-shone Trace Hughes's musical ability.

One by one, the congregation joined the singing. The music was so joyous, so upbeat and happy, that it was nearly irresistible. Amazingly, I heard several people clapping in time with the beat.

Was this the beginning of a new era at the First Baptist Church of Levi, staunch and loyal backbone of the community, dedicated and sincere followers of the Lord? As it turned out, Trace's sermon was just as unorthodox as his music.

"You know," he said, at last climbing onto the stage so everyone could see and hear him more easily, "I don't think a sermon has ever been preached that could outdo the Word of the Lord. So, this morning, I'm going to read to you from the Book of Deuteronomy, twenty-eighth chapter. I think it's something we should take to heart. It'd be good if every politician in state and federal governments could hear this at least once a week."

And, that's what he did. He read the whole chapter without leaving out a verse. Those ancient words became vivid and alive through the smoothness of Trace's voice. Even Grant, who had been sitting with his arms folded across his chest during the singing, relaxed and had an attentive look.

At the end of the chapter, Trace bowed his head, said a short prayer, and told us we were dismissed. The church buzzed like a hive of busy bees as we left, but I felt singularly blessed and refreshed by this unusual service. The only question I had was why this man, whom the Lord had showered with good looks and talent in abundance, was content to be the pastor of a small, countrified church in northeast Oklahoma?

Chapter 10

"What a crowd!" I said to Mom as we stood in the kitchen Sunday afternoon. "The notice Mort put in the paper helped bring 'em in. Or, we could have just skipped the ad and told Megaphone Mouth—I mean, Mort."

"Now, Darcy, you aren't giving Mort the benefit of the doubt. Maybe Ventris County is full of well-wishers."

Mort Bascomb, our newspaper's busy editor, had placed our housewarming notice on the front page, but most likely he told everyone in Ventris County as well. Mort completely dispelled that decidedly unfair adage about a woman not being able to keep secrets. Not that this housewarming was a secret, but Mort was the worst gossip I knew. Tales that didn't make it into the paper got around town anyway, by way of Mort's tendency to sit at Dilly's cafe and chitchat. Sure, he picked up lots of news items that way but, in the process, he offered quite a few rumors to sort of prime the pump, as he called it. Some of those stories, like the legend of Ben Ventris's gold, should have been kept quiet.

Jackson Conner paused in carrying a fresh platter of cookies out to the porch. "I don't think Mort means any harm though I agree, Darcy, he sometimes talks when he shouldn't."

"Maybe Mort is partly responsible for so many people," Mom said. "But there's the added attraction of wanting to meet our new preacher."

She took off her apron, folded it, and put it into a kitchen drawer. "Brother Trace looks like he's having a good time. I see he brought his guitar."

A group of our visitors sat around Trace Hughes, who was perched on the porch railing. His guitar music provided a nice background to the happy chatter of the guests.

Looking at the well-wishers who pretty much lined our wraparound porch, I felt sure that every person in Ventris County who wanted to come was here. As Mom said, some were strangers until tonight. She and I had greeted everyone, learning new names but, for the life of me, I couldn't remember all of them.

Tim Johnson, the new lawn person for the Jenkins twins, sat near them, evidently enjoying the conversation. He had a pleasant face. His laughter punctuated whatever story Miss Georgia was telling.

"You know, if Mr. Johnson wore a red suit, he would look like Santa Claus," I said to Mom. "He's got that pretty head of white hair and a full white beard."

"You're right," she agreed. "And, he seems so jolly, a happy addition to any crowd. I meant to tell you that I talked to him a few minutes ago about helping with the lawn. He said he'd be glad to do that."

Burke Hopkins, our quiet Cherokee friend from the country, sat in a lawn chair next to Grant's secretary, Doris Elroy. Hiram and Hattie Schuster sat on the porch steps, along with Viola Prender and Amy's husband Jack Miller. Jack was the quiet type; Amy was the outgoing half of that couple, but Amy seemed happy, and that must mean that Jack was a good husband.

Taking another look at Burke, I felt a niggling worry. He had always reminded me of Ben Ventris. Perhaps they were related? He looked tired, not the robust man I had known for years. Miss Georgia was right to retire him from mowing their lawn. The Methodist Church's octogenarian custodian, Gladys Holcutt, sat near Burke, a cookie in one hand and a glass of tea in the other.

Mort wasn't sitting; he was circulating, gathering, I felt sure, lots more juicy tidbits he could follow up on.

Grant and his deputy Jim Clendon were on duty and missing from our celebration. Jasper, too, was missing. I wondered if Grant had tracked him down yet.

Amy appeared from the guest room where she had stashed the supplies for our moonlight stroll.

"It's getting on toward dusk," she said, shaking the paper sack she carried. "I've got flashlights and maps here. Should I hand them out now?"

"No, wait'll I collect the trash from this bunch," Pat Harris answered, coming through the kitchen with a black garbage bag. "I'll just go out on the porch and pass this around. Everybody can dump their paper plates and cups in."

"It's a long time until dark," I said, glancing at the clock. "It is only six but you're right, those clouds make it an early dusk. I sure hope it doesn't rain out that wonderful stroll you are so set on, Amy. I don't think there will be any moonlight."

Amy giggled. "Oh, I don't know. A few thunder claps and lightning flashes will add to a ghost walk, don't you think? Especially when we get to that old cemetery."

Shaking my head, I decided to let Amy have her way if she preferred to call it a ghost walk. However, I was in charge of this little evening outing and I would make sure no one thought our acres were spooky.

Delving into the sack, I gathered a stack of handmade maps and took them to the front porch. Amy trailed behind me with the flashlights.

Several of our guests, including Burke and the three women who had ridden with him, opted to forego this activity in favor of going home.

As Burke came up to thank me for the invitation, he grasped my arm. "Darcy, I'm kind of worried about something. I can't tell you right now but I need to talk to you soon."

"Sure," I said, not liking the tension I saw in his dark eyes. "Come over any time or, if you'd rather, I can drive out to your house."

He nodded and turned to follow the Jenkins twins and Miss Holcutt to his truck. Some of the other guests took a look at the gathering clouds and declared they had had a great time but needed to do the milking or feed the chickens or be sure their dogs had food and water. Only about a dozen brave souls lingered for our ghost walk—I mean, evening stroll.

Raising my voice, I spoke to the group on the porch.

"We've had a great time this afternoon. Thank you all for coming. Amy is giving each person a flashlight and I'll be handing out maps that describe what we'll be seeing. We'll tour part of the grounds, starting with the herb garden behind our house. We'll follow the stepping stones through the herbs and down to the orchard, then across to an old cemetery that has been there for more than a hundred years, and finish by viewing Lee Creek from our bridge before returning to the house. Please go to the kitchen and have a glass of iced tea when we get back. I imagine after this jaunt, we'll need it."

"Ooh," said Viola, shivering. "I don't know about this. I've heard some scary tales about that cemetery. It's supposed to be haunted."

Shaking my head, I said, "Oh, for goodness sake, Mrs. Prender, I hope you aren't serious."

"Well, maybe, just a little, Darcy. You young'uns don't believe in old tales and superstitions, but there's got to be some truth to them."

Never in all the world would I tell Viola, but that deserted graveyard gave me the shivers and I avoided it when possible. It held a secret, unmarked grave. I remembered an incident that happened there a few months ago, the feeling that I was not alone when actually, I was. Quite alone. I think.

Trace Hughes smiled at Viola. "Remember to trust in the Lord, Mrs. Prender," he said. "We know that evil exists in this world, but I've never believed in ghosts."

"Thanks," I said. He stood very near, holding his flashlight and his map, his guitar once again slung over his shoulder. I didn't believe in ghosts either, but his presence was reassuring as well as something else—exciting, maybe?

"How is your burn?" he asked.

"It's healing nicely. That was so clumsy of me and embarrassing too."

Shaking his head, he said. "I feel responsible. I startled you."

Laughing, I touched his arm. "You are in no way responsible."

He put his hand over mine where it lay on his arm.

"Darcy, I've been wanting to talk to you. There's so much that I need to say but somehow, I can't find the right time or the right words."

"We'd better cross that bridge before Lee Creek starts to rise," Pat declared. "From the looks of those clouds, Darcy, we may have heavenly fireworks as a grand finale."

As if in answer, an ominous rumble of thunder growled in the distance.

"You're right, Pat," I said, grateful that she had changed the subject and offered a reason for me to move away from Trace and walk to the front of the little group.

Chapter 11

My faithful followers trooped through the house, out the back door and into the herb garden. Its tangy fragrance engulfed us as Mom, with Jackson at her side, beamed her flashlight onto the plants and explained the uses of various herbs and bushes.

"Lemon balm is good for tea," she said, "and it smells nice too. I've made an ointment from these gray mullein leaves. Sage can be made into an occasional hair rinse as well as used in the Thanksgiving stuffing. But, even though these lily of the valley have beautiful little bell-shaped blooms, they are poisonous, as are many herbs and flowers. It's best to have a healthy respect for them all and find out exactly what they will or won't do."

We moved slowly past Mom as she spoke, walking along the stepping stones, under branches of dogwood trees and to the old orchard.

Here, I stopped long enough to tell a story about gathering apples with my Granny Grace when I was a little girl, and the tasty applesauce she made. I remembered the scent of wood smoke mingled with the enticing aroma of the apples which simmered all day over a wood fire in the back yard.

We wound past the orchard's gnarled limbs and were in the cemetery.

"We aren't sure who these people are," I told my followers, shining my flashlight over the leaning gray headstones. "They may have been early settlers or perhaps Cherokee people."

Like earthbound fireflies, circles of light from the flashlights slid over the ground, causing shadows of the headstones to dance across the grass. The crowd fell silent.

A rising wind sighed through surrounding trees, and flashes of lightning shivered across the sky.

Something moved in the tree I stood under. An owl lifted off from a limb and flew silently away. Without meaning to, I had stopped beneath the cottonwood that grew close to the unmarked grave.

I did not believe in ghosts, but that lonely grave, with no name to mark it, gave me an uneasy feeling. Amy and her talk of a ghost walk! My childhood fear of the unknown, the coming storm, and the darkness of the night grasped me with invisible fingers. I was through with this. I wanted nothing more than the warmth and light of my mother's kitchen.From somewhere in the darkness of trees and undergrowth, a moan began. It grew louder until it sounded like the wail of someone in extreme pain. The hairs on my arm stood up, and I could not have moved if I had tried.

"What was that?" Viola whispered, breaking the paralysis.

Flashlights flickered through the trees and bushes as we searched for the source of the unearthly scream.

"I didn't know there were any left in these woods, but that, ladies and gentlemen, was the scream of a mountain lion. Some folks called them cougars or panthers." Mort's usually authoritative voice sounded shaky.

Mort was right. I had heard that chilling wail once before and would never forget the wild cat that slipped across the road in front of me in the dark woods not far from here. It was time to end this walk.

Doris spun on her heel. "I don't know about anybody else, but I'm going back to the house. Whether that was a mountain lion or...or whatever, I don't want to meet it."

Without warning, something dropped from the cottonwood which grew over that unmarked grave, something long and white.

Amy screamed.

A zigzag of lightning slashed the murky sky followed by a deafening peal of thunder. As if this were the signal, the clouds opened and rain poured down.

"Run!" Amy shouted.

"Don't panic!" I yelled. "You'll smack into something and fall. It's only a little rain."

No one heard me. Or, if they did, they paid no attention. Dodging tree limbs and rocks, the small group of adventurers bolted for the safety of their cars. Our evening stroll became a stormy stampede.

Chapter 12

The delicious aroma of perking coffee teased my eyes open on Monday morning. Glancing out of the window, I saw that the sun was not yet up, although the rooster in the chicken yard certainly was awake. Over and over, he voiced his enthusiasm for a new day.

Yesterday had been just as busy for my mother as it was for me. How did she maintain her energy and wake up early every morning? At the moment she was undoubtedly sitting downstairs with her cup of Folgers, her Bible open on the kitchen table.

"I need to have my daily spiritual vitamins," she had told me more than once.

Her complete confidence in God made more and more sense to me. After Jake's death, and actually even before his death, God seemed to be far away. Why had the Lord taken my husband, this man I loved with all my heart, and left me to struggle on without him? It was a slow process, but, little by little, I was learning to trust God again.

Sometimes, my life with Jake seemed unreal, as if it had never happened or had been a dream. At other times, something happened that brought him sharply into focus. Life with Jake had been exciting and fun. His impromptu bouquets of flowers, a mysterious drive to a new place he had found for a moonlight dinner, trips to the seashore or to the mountains, all of these had been part of those magical years.

Immediately, our new preacher popped into my mind. Without doubt, Trace was attractive and intriguing. However, I did not want to become entangled in an emotional triangle. Grant loved me—I knew he did—and I loved Grant too. Unbidden, a little voice seemed to whisper, "But, how much, Darcy?"

Scooting Jethro off my pillow, I yawned, stretched, and swung my feet to the floor. Enough quandaries. I needed at least two cups of coffee for my brain to function properly. Besides, there were some things I wanted to discuss with my mother.

Jethro glared at me and stalked in regal dignity into the hall. That cat must have been descended from royalty. Such an attitude!

Going to my closet, I reached for a pair of blue jeans and a red-and-white striped sleeveless shirt. I pulled my hair into a high ponytail, slipped into some flip-flops and hurried downstairs.

"Good morning, Sleepyhead," Mom said, smiling. She closed her Bible, went to the cabinet and took down another cup.

I filled the cup and sat down. "It really isn't so late. It's just that you are an early bird."

"You know how it is. Once my eyes pop open, there's no getting them shut again. Besides, I wanted to think about a few things and pray. Prayer is the best way to start the day."

Ah. That first sip of Folgers tasted as good as it smelled.

"I want to talk to you too, Mom. The housewarming went off well, in spite of the storm, don't you think?"

She nodded. "Yes. I enjoyed having everyone here, seeing old friends and meeting new ones, but taking that evening stroll might not have been such a good idea."

"It was Amy's plan. She thought it would be interesting. And, it was certainly that. Do you think that was really the scream of a mountain lion we heard? It sounded awfully close."

"Yes, I do," Mom said. "We know some still live in these parts, although lots of people think they are all gone."

"Something else happened on that ill-fated walk. Did you think you saw something white drop out of the cottonwood or was that my imagination?"

Mom laughed. "Yes, I saw it, but I'm pretty sure it was just a dead limb that fell off when a gust of wind caught it."

Swallowing my coffee, I said, "You're probably right but I doubt that any of our little group of explorers will believe it."

"They did look scared when they got back to the house. I noticed that most of them left pretty quickly."

"I've never liked that old graveyard," I said. "I know it's silly but it gives me the shivers. Maybe it's that one lonely grave without any headstone. Do you think we should put something up to mark that grave?"

Mom looked down at her coffee cup and spoke in a low voice, "That's a good idea. Everyone deserves to have their final resting place remembered. I don't believe in ghosts, Darcy. I think the only haunts in that cemetery would be the bad memories associated with it. Cemeteries are lonely, sad places and for that reason, I don't like to go to them."

She was silent for so long, I was afraid my talk of unmarked graves had upset her. If she was going to worry about it, I would drop the subject. Forcing myself to sound a lot cheerier than I felt, I grinned and said, "When that limb blew off the tree, it was the last straw! Notwithstanding the mountain lion and the spookiness and the rain that caught us, it was a great day and evening, with hearing Trace preach and having everyone out here last night."

My mother gave me what I've always called her straight look. I became familiar with it as a teen when I stayed out too late on a date and she waited up for me.

"What do you think about our new preacher?" she asked.

"Trace Hughes? Well, um, I think he's very talented. He can sure play a mean guitar and he has a nice voice."

"And a charming Southern drawl and courtly manners. It's too bad that Grant couldn't be here last night."

My face began to feel uncomfortably warm.

"Speaking of Grant, I wonder if he ever caught up with Jasper?" I asked, changing the subject abruptly.

"Pat said he hasn't. I'm really sorry that boy decided to go streeling off somewhere just at the time that poor man was found dead at Old String's place," Mom said. "Especially since his knife was found there. Makes him look guilty."

The word "streeling" brought back memories.

Grinning, I said, "I haven't heard 'streeling' since Dad used to tell me, when I was a kid, not to go streeling off and get lost."

Mom smiled. "I guess he could have said not to go roaming off or strolling off. I learned lots of Irish words after I married Andy Tucker."

"Dad was Irish, through and through. But getting back to Jasper, surely you don't think he killed that poor man?"

Mom snorted and got up to refill her cup. "No, I sure don't. I've known Jasper all his life and although he may be a trifle strange, there's not a mean bone in his body."

I toyed with my cup, turning it around in a circle as I thought through my next words.

"Somebody, though, killed the man. Grant thinks it was a knife wound, and I'm afraid he is sure it was Jasper's knife. He hasn't told me Doc McCauley's verdict or if they've found out the dead man's name. What if…" I looked up at Mom standing by the stove. I didn't want to scare her but she needed to be more suspicious. She was entirely too trusting.

"Well," Mom interrupted, "I think it was probably a drifter, somebody passing through, maybe somebody the dead man had met who didn't like him. It may be that we'll never know any more about it."

Scooting back my chair, I stood up to face her. "But, what if it was somebody here in Levi? In fact, Mom, what if the murderer was one of the people here at our housewarming last night?"

She pressed her index finger against the side of her mouth, a habit she had when she was upset. "I just can't believe that somebody with meanness on their mind would have dared come out in public to a get-together. I'd think he would be many miles away by now."

"You know that some of our guests were strangers. Maybe they came to hear what was being said about the murder, or…or something."

"Next, you'll be telling me the killer was somebody we know, one of our neighbors or friends," Mom scoffed.

"And, that is a possibility. It has certainly happened before," I said.

Mom shook her head. "Maybe you should let well enough alone, dear daughter. I'm sure Grant and Jim will find out who killed that poor man. You remember, Darcy, that each time we've dipped our oar into a problem here in town, we've found ourselves in a heap of trouble."

"I've been thinking about something falling out of the tree at the old cemetery last night, and my feeling that I wasn't alone. What if somebody was there and heard us coming and climbed that tree? What if he knocked down a limb and that's what fell?"

Mom shook her head and sighed. "You won't be satisfied until you go back to the cemetery and check it out. I don't think anybody was up in that tree. I think the wind blew the limb down. But, if you want to go back and look around, I'll go with you."

As it turned out, we didn't have time to follow through on our good intentions. Mom can dish up a breakfast that cannot be ignored. I had finished bacon, blueberry pancakes, orange juice, and coffee, loaded the dishes into the dishwasher, and was about to head out the door to the cemetery when the phone rang. It was Grant's secretary, Doris Elroy, and she had a strange request.

Chapter 13

"Darcy, Grant asked me to have you and Miss Flora meet him at Miss Sugar's. He wouldn't tell me why. He just said it was important. I know it's awfully early. Sorry."

Doris Elroy's normally calm voice held a note of impatience. Was she aggravated with her boss? Usually, Doris was Grant's staunch supporter.

Lulabelle Shuggart was the owner, operator and general compassion-giver at Shuggart's Funeral Home. Plump, bespectacled, and white-haired, she exuded sympathy, concern, and competence. It was no wonder that everyone in town shortened her last name to Sugar. There had been a Shuggart's Funeral Home in Levi since time immemorial. Miss Lulabelle Shuggart was the third generation of her family in the business of burying Ventris County's dear departed. Now her nephew and his son were also involved. Shuggart's would be in the grave business for years to come. It was odd, what I felt upon coming face to face with Miss Sugar. I associated her with my father's funeral and sadness, but, at the same time, she radiated a feeling of comfort. Other than that, I didn't know much about Lulabelle Shuggart. There was a rumor that she had been in love once, but the young man had a change of heart. Humans are strange people.

Glancing at the clock, I said, "That's all right, Doris. We are early risers. Why does Grant want us to go to the funeral home, of all places?"

"He wouldn't tell me why, but he said he's going out to Miss Pat's first. I gathered he is bringing her to the funeral home and wants you to be there in case Pat needs you. At 8:30, he said."

"Pat? Pat Harris?" I asked.

Mom hurried to the phone. "Is it Pat? Is she sick?"

"Yes, Pat Harris," Doris said. "I don't know what to make of it, Darcy. I don't think Grant has ever located Jasper. Maybe…no, we won't think the worst."

A cold dread settled around my heart. I had to swallow a couple of times before I could answer. "Sure, Doris, we'll be there."

"What in the world is going on?" Mom asked as I replaced the receiver.

"Grant wants us to meet him and Pat at Miss Sugar's at 8:30. Doris didn't know why."

"Oh, no! Maybe it's Jasper. Oh, surely not. Grant wouldn't be bringing Pat to the funeral home unless…unless it was to identify him." Mom's voice sank to a whisper.

Pouring two more cups of coffee, I set them on the table and guided Mom to a chair. Her hands were shaking.

"Grant wouldn't break the news to us this way," I said, as we faced each other at the table. "He would phone us himself and not ask Doris to phone, or he would come to the house. No, it can't be Jasper."

I tried to sound reassuring, but my coffee sloshed out of my cup as I raised it to my lips. I guessed my own face was as pale as my mother's.

Grant's white Ford truck was parked in front of Shuggart's when Mom and I arrived. Inside the door of the funeral home, Miss Sugar met us.

She hugged Mom, then took my icy hands in her warm ones and smiled.

I couldn't ask the question I was burning to know. Were we there because Jasper lay in one of the slumber rooms? Glancing at Mom, I saw that she was holding herself stiff and silent, evidently unwilling to ask Miss Sugar if Pat's son was dead. We were both afraid of the answer.

"Now, just don't you all be upset," Miss Sugar said. "It's going to be all right. I don't know what Grant told you, but you are going to be a real strength for Pat. I know you are. Come on into the back parlor. Would you like a cup of coffee? A glass of tea?"

Shaking my head, Mom and I followed Miss Sugar through a short hall and into a small room. The lighting was dim; the sofa and chairs were upholstered in some sort of velvety purple brocade. The room seemed stuffy and closed in. I did not like it even though Miss Sugar was the epitome of strength and hospitality.

Neither Mom nor I sat down. We were standing facing the door when Pat came in, closely followed by Grant. When she saw us, tears formed in her eyes and ran down her cheeks. Mom wrapped her arms around her.

My heart hammering in my throat, I looked questioningly at Grant. He shook his head and managed a half smile.

"Who is it, Grant?" I whispered. "Is it...is it Jasper?"

"No, no. It isn't Jasper," Grant answered.

"It's Walter!" Pat burst out. "It's Walter. I haven't seen him for about twenty years and now he's back and he's dead!"

"Walter?" I asked.

Mom led Pat to the sofa and sat down beside her.

"Walter is Pat's husband," Mom said in a quiet voice. "Jasper's father."

Miss Sugar supplied Pat with a box of tissues then tiptoed out of the room. We all waited until she calmed down, blew her nose, and looked at each of us.

"Grant said Doc McCauley was pretty sure it was Walter but they didn't have any dental records. I don't think that man went to a dentist once in his life. He's changed a lot in twenty years but I'd know him anywhere even..." The tears started again. "Even though he's dead."

"Now, Pat," Mom said, "I know you're shocked. Death is not a welcome visitor at any time, but you're going to make yourself sick. You've told me over and over that you were well rid of him. Remember? He left you and Jasper to fend for yourselves and didn't even send word where he was or anything. Try to get hold of yourself."

Wiping her eyes, Pat blew her nose and nodded.

"You're right, Flora. It's just that when I saw him, I realized how pitiful he looked and how I was sorry it all ended this way." She snuffled. "Of course I don't love him anymore."

"But it hurts anyhow, doesn't it?" Mom asked, her voice as soft as the sunlight on new leaves.

This brought a fresh onslaught of tears from Pat.

Grant turned his hat around in his hands and shuffled his feet. "Miss Pat, I'm really sorry to grieve you, but you're the only one who could positively identify Walter Harris. When you are able, I'd like for Miss Flora to take you home. Darcy, would you step outside for a minute?"

The warmth of the summer day after the cloying atmosphere inside felt good as we walked out of the funeral home. I took a deep breath of rain-washed air and turned to Grant.

"What does all this mean?" I asked.

"Here's what I know, Darcy. Walter Harris had a reason for coming back home after all this time. I don't know what that reason was. You said when he recognized Miss Flora, he bolted. Jasper's knife was found close to Walter's body. Jasper is missing. Now, that sounds like guilt to me."

"But Grant, Walter was Jasper's father. He wouldn't kill his own father!"

Grant's eyebrows drew down and his voice sounded grim.

"Wouldn't he? You know Jasper's temper. It flares up and then is gone. What if he hated his father for leaving him all those years ago? What if Jasper was out wandering through the woods and went into Old String's hut to get out of the rain? What if Walter came in, recognized Jasper, and told him he was his long-lost daddy? Jasper might have stabbed him before he thought things through, then got scared and ran off."

I hated to admit it, but Grant's theory made sense. A heavy weight seemed to settle on my shoulders. What would Pat do if she lost her son as well as that no-good husband?

I glanced at the funeral home door as Mom and Pat came through it.

Grant replaced his hat and tipped my chin up with his forefinger. "Thanks for coming in, Darcy. You and Miss Flora take Miss Pat on home, okay?"

"Sure, Grant," I said and watched him stride to his truck. We would take Miss Pat home with us first. I had the feeling that by the end of the day, both Mom and Miss Pat were going to be drained of all energy. I hoped that, in Mom's devotion time this morning, she asked for strength. In dealing with her friend, she would need it.

Chapter 14

Amazingly, as Pat sat at the dining table with us, she became calm.

"You know, I'm sorry that Walter is dead," she told Mom. "But I'm kind of relieved, too, that the worry has ended. I've wondered all these years where he was, what kind of life he had. I'll probably never know the answers to those things, but at least I know where he is now and I won't keep looking for him to come back."

Sighing, Pat took another sip of coffee then carried her cup to the sink.

Turning to Mom, she said, "If you'll drive me out to my house, Flora, I think I'd like to lie down for a bit. Now if my son would just come home!"

After she returned from Pat's house, Mom and I sat on the porch swing and drank in the quiet of a lazy summer day. Jethro lay on a cushioned porch chair, his nose between his paws. Actually, a summer day in Oklahoma is never quiet. The cicadas grated their gravelly song and down by Lee Creek a bullfrog voiced his approval of his lot in life. A mockingbird sang in an oak and some small, secretive animal scuttled through the underbrush.

"We've got to find Jasper," I told Mom.

"Just how do you think we should go about that?" she asked.

I pushed the swing with my toe.

"I'm not sure. I've been thinking about it. We have to set a trap of a sort, some way to lure him out. He must be around here, somewhere close. He would never leave his mother unguarded."

Mom nodded. "You're right. Jasper is protective of Pat."

We were interrupted by the sound of an approaching vehicle. An old truck chugged up the hill and across the bridge.

"That looks like Burke Hopkins's truck," Mom said, shading her eyes with her hand.

We stood up to meet Burke as he parked in the driveway, trudged across the yard and climbed the porch steps, a sack in his hand, and his dog Ranger at his heels.

"Burke! How nice to see you," Mom said, smiling. "Come and join us." She motioned toward one of the porch chairs.

"I'll bring out some iced tea," I said.

Jethro jumped to the floor and scooted into the house ahead of me.

"Thanks." Burke took off his cap, set the brown paper sack beside him, and wiped his forehead with a neatly folded white handkerchief. "Feels mighty good to sit for a spell. Warm day and the rain we've had makes it kind of muggy."

With a heavy sigh, Ranger lay down at his feet.

I brought the tea. Burke's hand, as he took the glass, shook. What was up with our old friend?

"How are those hens I gave you?" Burke asked. "Any of them in the family way yet?"

"One," Mom answered. "She's not the best-tempered gal in the flock, but maybe she'll be a good mother."

For a few seconds, we sat listening to the slow squeaking of the porch swing and the sounds of summer. Burke's usual smile was gone. Indeed, he was looking older than he had Sunday night.

Finally, Burke cleared his throat and set his glass on the porch beside his sack.

"I've got something I need to tell both of you," he began. "I don't rightly know how to do it, though. I'm not even sure that I should, but…"

His voice trailed off as he squinted down the hill at Lee Creek sparkling in the sun.

I fidgeted. What on earth was bearing on his mind? Did he have some information about Pat's husband?

Finally, the silence got to me. "Mr. Hopkins, do you know who killed Walter Harris?"

"Walter?" His look of surprise was genuine. "Are you saying the dead man you found is Walter Harris, Jasper's pa?"

I nodded. "Sorry. I forgot that you probably hadn't heard yet."

"No, I hadn't," Burke said thoughtfully. "I haven't seen Walter since he left. Hate to say it, but about the only thing I remember about him was that he never was very work brittle."

Mom nodded. "You mean he was kind of lazy and no-account for working."

"That's what I mean," Burke said. "I wonder why he came back? No, what I've got to say doesn't have anything to do with poor old Walter and I don't know how to edge up on it so I'll just spit it out."

In my opinion, Burke was a master edger. He was very good at beating around the bush. I would have to try to curb my impatience.

"I've got in a habit of going over to Tahlequah every so often to visit old friends in a nursing home there," he began slowly.

I knew that Burke, who was Cherokee, went to the capital of the Cherokee Nation frequently, to visit or to take a neighbor to the courthouse to check out a land deed. There wasn't a kinder soul in Ventris County than Burke.

He gazed at a hawk sitting on the top limb of a nearby sycamore. "Well, there was one particular fellow I always visited. He was a World War II vet. Mind was as sharp as my hunting knife. He was missing a leg, from the war. He was Cherokee too and we seemed to have a lot in common. He had been gone from Oklahoma for quite some time and only recently came back. He said he wanted to spend his final days in his hometown."

"Who was this fellow?" I interrupted. "You're talking in past tense. Did he die?"

Burke frowned. "Now, hold your horses, Darcy. I'm gettin' to that. For a long time, I didn't know his last name. Just knew him as Jeff. Finally, he told me his name and the name of the girl he had planned to marry, a long, long time ago. And then, next time I went to visit, he was gone. Dead. Died in his sleep, Darcy, so I don't think there's a mystery there."

There had to be more to Burke's story. Why should it be hard to tell us about visiting with a World War II soldier? And, sad as it was, his death would surely not have been unexpected. Why didn't Burke quit swirling the ice in his glass and get on with it?

Burke reached down and patted Ranger's head. The old dog thumped his tail on the porch in appreciation. "Jeff didn't own much of this world's goods. Oh, there was the usual nursing home stuff but other than that, he had just one piece of furniture in his room, an old treadle sewing machine kind of toward the back of the room. He said it had belonged to his mother and a cousin kept it for years. When he went to see this cousin, just before she died, she gave it back to him. A long time ago, Jeff meant to give it to the girl he was going to marry. He was mighty particular with that sewing machine. He'd roll his wheel chair over to it and dust it every day."

Burke paused and shook his head.

"He had a picture sitting in a frame on top of the sewing machine, an old, faded picture of himself when he was just a young man, in his soldier's uniform. His intended was in the picture too. They made a mighty handsome pair, smiling and happy, not knowin' what lay ahead for either of them. Which, come to think of it, was probably just as well."

"Did he marry her?" Mom asked. "Is there a happy ending to this story, Burke?"

"Depends on how you look at it," he said. "Jeff told me his plane had been shot down in the war and he was captured. Then, he was in a hospital in France for a long time. His own folks thought he was dead. For a time, he didn't remember much, not even who he was. During those years, his parents died, not knowing he was still alive, and he became bitter about life in general. After the war, he threw in with a sorry lot up north some'eres and got in trouble with the law for bank robbery, spent some time in jail."

Shaking her head, Mom said slowly, "That sure is a sad story. What about Jeff's fiancée? Didn't he want to see her again, tell her he was alive?"

Burke took a deep breath, his shoulders rising and falling. He shook his head.

"He said that he'd left her as a young fellow, with a good outlook on life and she deserved more than a cripple. Then, after his stint as an outlaw, he was ashamed to face her. Along the way, he found the Lord and became a Christian, but he said it was better that his sweetheart thought he was dead."

A suspicion began in the back of my mind. A preposterous idea was taking shape. Unshed tears felt hot behind my eyelids.

"What was Jeff's last name, Burke?" I whispered.

"Now, let me finish up, Darcy. Jeff told me his name and his sweetheart's name. And then I got a good look at that picture he had sittin' on top of the sewing machine. He made me promise not to tell her that he was alive. He wanted her to remember him as the young man he used to be, all full of life and hopes and dreams."

Reaching into the sack he had brought with him, Burke pulled out an old picture and handed it to Mom. The porch swing stilled. Mom stared at the two people in the photograph, her brow furrowed. Quickly, I slid closer and took her hand in mine.

She looked up at me, her eyes wide and wondering. "It's Miss Georgia Jenkins and a young man in uniform," she said. Then she looked directly at Burke. "Are you telling me that the man in this picture, this Jeff that you got to know at the nursing home, is actually Jefferson Thorne?"

My breath caught in my throat. Mom had known for some time that Granny Grace had adopted her. Recently, we found out Miss Georgia was her mother. I remembered Miss Georgia's tears as she told Mom the pain she had felt at giving her up. She said that Mom's father was a soldier named Jefferson Thorne, but Miss Georgia thought he had been killed during the war.

Burke nodded, his eyes never leaving Mom's face. "Yes, Flora, that was Jeff's full name. The nursing home folks said that he wanted me to have the sewing machine and that picture he kept sittin' on top of it. I took them, but I don't want them. So, they are yours. You can decide whether you want Miss Georgia to know the story I've told you. It's not for me to say."

Burke smiled and got to his feet. Ranger scrambled up and stood looking at him. "I feel better now that I've gotten that load off my chest. Maybe that's selfish of me, 'cause I've just shifted it onto the both of you. Darcy, if you'll give me a hand, I believe we can tote that machine into your house."

Chapter 15

My mother sat gazing at the faded photograph. This revelation of Burke's brought memories of the day last winter when she and I had confronted Miss Georgia and learned the truth about Mom's birth.

"So, what do you think, Mom?" I asked, as we sat at the hundred-year-old table, our cups of untasted coffee in front of us.

She didn't look up from the picture. "About what?"

"About Burke's story and Jefferson Thorne," I said. "Are you going to tell Miss Georgia and take her the sewing machine and picture?" Slowly, Mom shook her head. "I don't think so. She has her memories of a young Jeff Thorne, handsome, full of the joy of life. She never married, so she must have loved him very much."

"It didn't sound like he ever married either," I said.

She sighed and looked at me. "No, he didn't. But, if I tell Miss Georgia that he didn't die in the war and was living only a few miles from her and didn't contact her, it will hurt her all over again. She has come to terms with her past and this would really be a shock."

I nodded. "We'll have to hide that picture. What are you going to do with the sewing machine?"

"I don't know. Miss Georgia probably wouldn't recognize it. Maybe she never saw it, but yes, I'll put the photograph away somewhere."

"So Burke knows that Jeff Thorne was your father? Is that why he brought those things to you?"

"Of course he does. So far as I know, nobody but Miss Carolina, Miss Georgia, you and I are sure that Miss Georgia gave birth to me. It's not anything I'm ashamed of but it's just kind of private. There'd be people who would condemn Miss Georgia or make some sort of remark if it was common knowledge, and I guess it's really nobody else's business," Mom said. "Burke figured it out, but he'd never say so."

"And, how about you, Mom? Are you okay with all this information? Did Burke upset you terribly?"

She shook her head and smiled. "No, not really. I've wondered about my birth father ever since I knew that I was adopted. Now, I know what he looked like and what happened to him. I sure wish I could have met him, but a chapter in my life has ended so I can quit wondering about a lot of things. There's one thing, though, that I still wonder about."

She closed her eyes for a second then continued.

"I just wish I knew for sure, for sure and certain that Jeff meant to marry Miss Georgia. I hope he did, but those war years were turbulent times. People didn't always think clearly when faced with the prospect of a long separation. When Jeff left, did he really intend to marry her, or was the love all on her side?"

It would have been nice if Burke could have answered that question for us, but there was no proof that Jeff Thorne was an honorable man. I hoped he was, but his choice to live the life of an outlaw didn't sound honorable.

"I'm sure he meant to come back home and marry her," I told Mom. "He kept the sewing machine and their picture all these years. War changes people, you know, and what Burke told us about Jeff's reasons not to make himself known makes sense. If I put myself in Jeff's place, I might have done the same."

Shaking her head, Mom said, "I choose to believe the best about both of my birth parents. I think Jeff must have been a good man. I hope he was."

Gathering our cups, I emptied them into the sink and poured fresh coffee.

"Levi is a small town," I said, "and a stranger might think everyone here lives a peaceful, open life, but I believe we have as many secrets as we have trees. This quiet surface is deceptive."

Mom nodded as I set fresh coffee in front of her. "Yes. Nobody would ever guess some of the things that have gone on. I was just thinking back to last winter and to the eight of us, six of our closest friends, and Mama Grace's journal. That journal held some pretty tough things, secrets that hadn't seen the light of day for a long time. I guess you could call us the circle of silence because I trust every one of those people, Miss Georgia and Miss Carolina, Burke, Grant, Pat, and Jackson not to breathe a word that Mama wrote."

"I agree," I said, remembering the sadness I had felt as I read my grandmother's journal entry describing a terrible first marriage and how it ended. I could almost smell the wood smoke from the fireplace and see the snow, which had been deep on the ground at our house in town as I read Granny Grace's words. Again, I felt the support and empathy from each person gathered to hear the journal read. Our friends might be a circle of silence, but they were also a warm and supportive group.

Not only had Granny Grace written about her first husband, Markham Cauldfell, she had recounted a murder committed by Judge Jenkins and the fact that not many people, including the sheriff, ever knew about it. Yes, Levi had its secrets, and it seemed that my own family had a share in them.

Laying the picture aside, Mom gazed at me, her eyes bright with unshed tears.

"You know, Darcy, until this past year, I thought your heritage was a pretty good one. There never were better parents nor more sincere Christians than George and Grace Daniels. Now, I've learned that I was born out of wedlock and my birth father was, at one time, a criminal. Besides that, Mama sure didn't show good sense when she married that Markham Cauldfell fellow. Your natural great-grandfather, Judge

Jenkins, killed a man and kept it a secret. At best, I'd say your heritage is a grave one."

My mother's tears shook me to the core. One of Dad's many sayings was, "Sometimes you have to laugh to keep from crying." So, I did the only thing I could think of to break the aura of gloom that threatened to settle around us. I laughed.

That worked! Eyes snapping, Mom said, "My goodness, Darcy! Have you lost your senses? What under the sun is funny about all this?"

Reaching across the table, I squeezed her hand. "Oh, Mom, think of it! Think of the people we've always looked up to, so respectable and virtuous, so God-fearing and honest. How'd they get that way? Maybe it's because they came through some tough times. Maybe it's because they strayed from the Lord and He brought them back and they've experienced God's grace first hand. I'd say our family is a shining example of God's forgiveness. They sinned, they repented, and they held up their heads and kept going. They sure didn't knuckle under in shame and defeat, and we won't either! I'm pretty proud of them all!"

Slowly, Mom smiled. It was like sunshine breaking through clouds. Then she began to laugh too.

"You're right, Darcy. And I'll bet everybody has something they'd just as soon the world didn't know. I guess you've got a pretty good heritage after all. We're the gold standard of what the Lord can do. 'When thou walkest through the fire…'" she murmured.

Maybe it was our way of dealing with Burke's sensational story. Maybe we had downed too much tea and coffee; whatever the reason, we both laughed until we cried. Jethro slipped off his cushioned chair, and, with a questioning glance at us, slunk into the living room. We laughed until the ceiling light flickered and caused us to glance out the window. It looked like another storm was coming.

Chapter 16

The afternoon had grown so dark that, inside the house, it almost seemed like night. Three things happened simultaneously: lightning flashed, the lights blinked off, and the front door rattled.

My heart flip-flopped and landed in my throat. Mom sat frozen in her chair. This was eerily similar to the night when Walter Harris came to our door. Once again, someone knocked—loudly.

"I'll go," I said. "You stay here."

"No. I'm coming too," Mom replied.

Peering through the front window, I shivered with a strange feeling of déjà vu. I recognized the figure on the porch and I feared him not at all.

"Jasper Harris!" I yelled, yanking open the door.

Mom grasped him by his soggy arm. "What are you doing? Don't you know that your mother is worried sick about you and Grant Hendley is looking for you?"

With his hair plastered to his forehead and his clothes dripping rain, Jasper was a spooky reminder of the elder Harris who had stood in this very spot not long ago.

Closing the door behind him, I crossed my arms over my chest and used the sternest voice I could muster.

"All right, Jasper, what gives?"

Mom disappeared into the bathroom and came back holding a towel.

"Darcy, give the boy a chance. He's half drowned. Dry off, Jasper, then come into the kitchen and have something to eat. I imagine you are starving."

Sidling away from me, Jasper took the towel.

"Thanks, Miss Flora. Yes, I'm right hungry," he said.

Mom bustled around the kitchen and soon had peanut butter and jelly sandwiches, a couple of apples, two pieces of cherry pie, and a glass of milk on the table for our impromptu guest.

Jasper wasted no time digging in.

"You aren't finished, are you, Jasper?" Mom asked when he stopped eating after only half the food was gone.

He wiped his mouth and grinned. "I'm full to the brim, Miss Flora, but I'll save the rest for later. Thanks a lot! Do you mind if I take it with me? And, do you think I could have another glass of milk poured into a jar that I could take?"

Mom looked puzzled but nodded. "Sure, I can fix it up for you but Jasper, aren't you going home now? Why are you hiding?"

Jasper's forehead wrinkled as he gazed at Mom. "I can't go home 'cause Darcy's friend, Grant the sheriff, thinks I killed my pa, and Mom would cry and beg me to talk to Grant. I saw it in the paper, Miss Flora. I know that my pa is dead and folks think I done it."

"Now, look, Jasper," I began, "you don't want to be a fugitive from the law. If you didn't kill your father, and I don't think you did, it is best for you to go to Grant and tell him."

Shaking his head so vigorously that his wet blond hair stood out, he scowled at me. "You don't know nothin'. I didn't kill nobody. I ain't got no way of provin' it though. And, Mort wrote in that newspaper of his that my knife was found beside Pa."

"Now, now," Mom said soothingly, "don't get excited, Jasper. Why don't you tell us what really happened while I put this food in a sack?"

Mort and his mega mouth! I imagined Grant was pretty unhappy that Mort mentioned the knife.

Laying my hand on her arm, I said, "Mom, do you realize you are helping Jasper evade the law? I don't know how Grant will look at that, but I think it could be called aiding and abetting."

"For goodness sake, Darcy," she said, "Jasper is a neighbor, Pat's son. I've known this boy all his life and he's hungry, needing food. He isn't a fugitive. Besides, what Grant doesn't know won't hurt him."

It might, however, hurt us if Grant were to find out we befriended Jasper and helped him stay in hiding by feeding him. Mom had that stubborn look on her face and I knew that it was useless to argue.

"Okay, Jasper, talk," I said. "Tell us your version of what happened on that night your father wound up dead outside of Old String's shack."

Rain poured from the stormy skies, lightning skittered across the heavens, and in the semi-darkness, Jasper looked as if he might bolt at any second. He glanced around the kitchen like a caged animal. Mom, I noticed, was taking her time about getting his food together. I felt sure she was using a delaying tactic to keep him talking.

"Well..." he cleared his throat. "It was rainin', you know, and the rain caught me out in the woods. I was owling and..."

"Jasper!" I interrupted. "I didn't know you were into owling. That's interesting."

Owling was an activity I wanted to try some moonlit night, if it ever stopped raining long enough for the moon to show its face. I loved owls, and searching for them and cataloging what kind and how many would be a fascinating activity.

He looked offended. "Sure, I am, Darcy. They're mighty neat birds. Anyway, the rain came up and I didn't have time to get back to the house so I ducked into Old String's place until the storm let up. Hurry, Miss Flora, will you?" he asked, fidgeting in his chair.

"Go on," I prompted as Mom lit a chunky candle and set it on the table.

"Old String's is a mighty good place for a hideout, or at least it was. That storm was loud and lasted a while. I picked up a stick off the floor and started whittling a whistle out of it, just to pass the time. I guess I wasn't the only one lookin' to get out of the rain that night. I hadn't been there long when a man came runnin' in. I shone my flashlight on his face, but he grabbed it and turned it on me. I didn't like that one bit, I tell you."

Jasper stared down at his plate, frowning as he remembered. "Anyway, he looked me over and, real slow, he said, 'I know you. You're my son Jasper.'"

"And then I remembered a little bit of what my pa looked like. Once I saw an old picture Mom had of him, so I knew he was tellin' the truth. He said something about maybe he had made a mistake and he said he wanted to explain somethin' to me."

Jasper shook his head, his face turning red. "I didn't want to hear nothin' he had to say. If he wanted to say he was sorry for runnin' off and leavin' Mom and me, it was too late. I got up and ran back out into the rain. I guess I must have dropped my knife."

Mom nodded. "Yes, you did and I'm sure sorry about that, Jasper. Somebody found it and killed Walter. I know it wasn't you, but it makes you look guilty."

We three sat staring at the sputtering candle, rain pounding the house and thunder rattling the dishes in the cabinet.

"You'd better wait here until this weather lets up," Mom said.

That brought Jasper to life. He shoved his chair away from the table, grabbed the sack of food, and stood up. "No, I can't. I've gotta go. Don't worry, Miss Flora, I've got some place to get out of the rain. Tell Mom not to worry. Thanks for the food."

And he was gone, out of the door and off the porch. The rain, like a gray curtain, closed around him, shutting him from our sight.

Chapter 17

The rain let up around midnight. I knew the time because I could not sleep and kept looking at the clock beside my bed. Not having that problem, Jethro snoozed soundly, curled on the pillow next to my head.

People and events circled through my mind like horses on a carousel, round and round, over and over: Walter Harris lying dead outside of Old String's house, Trace Hughes and his motorcycle and the image of him in church playing his guitar and singing.

I punched my pillow savagely and Jethro raised his head. If only our new preacher did not remind me of Jake! I certainly did not want to be attracted to this handsome, talented stranger.

Scenes from the open house Sunday spun through my thoughts. Shivering, I felt again the strange sense of unease I felt at the old cemetery. The trip to the Shuggart Funeral Home was unnerving, and was there really a mysterious prowler at the Jenkins home? Were the two ladies imagining things?

Burke's visit and his revelation about Jefferson Thorne was in my mix of jumbled thoughts. To top it off, Jasper showed up here on our front porch, much as his father had, which put Mom and me in the uncomfortable position of keeping a secret from Grant.

Try as I might, my mind would not shut off. I repeated Bible verses; I prayed and tried to remember happy scenes from my childhood. Nothing worked. Sleep would not come.

At last, I threw back the sheet and padded softly downstairs to the kitchen. Maybe a cup of chamomile tea made from the herb in Mom's garden would help me sleep.

Putting the kettle on a burner, I shook some dried tea into an infuser and waited for the water to heat. Going to the old sewing machine, I brought the photograph of my grandparents back to the table and sat staring at it. My grandfather had been a handsome man and, in his World War II uniform, looked dashing and exciting. How sad that he had been so near and we never knew him.

The teakettle whistled, and I got up to pour water over the infuser. Somewhere in a nearby tree, an owl hooted. Farther away, another answered him with the exact pattern of "Whoos." The owls may have been saying that the rain was over, for a while at least. This was the rainiest July on record. Did the weather pattern have anything to do with the unnerving events of the past few days? Mankind was, after all, much affected by weather.

"Stop it!" I said aloud. Such thoughts led to believing in superstitions, and I didn't—believe in superstitions, that is. Long ago my Cherokee and Irish ancestors had tried to explain unusual happenings by making up legends or stories. While these were interesting and fun to read, I would count on the Lord to be with us and protect us. How many times in the Book of Joshua did He tell us to fear not?

Removing the infuser from the cup, I added a dollop of honey and carried my tea to the dining table.

Sometimes I missed my job at The Dallas Morning News. Being an investigative reporter had led me into danger, but it certainly kept me busy. Maybe I should talk to Mort about a job on his newspaper. Goodness knew, Mort needed someone to report news, not gossip. If he had not mentioned Jasper's knife being found at Old String's place, Jasper might not be in hiding from the law. Discretion was not Mort's strong suit.

Finishing my tea, I replaced the old picture on the sewing machine and glanced out of the window. Scudding clouds played hide-and-seek with the moon. The rain was definitely over. I made a decision as I looked out at the dark shapes of trees. Today I would go to Levi's newspaper office and see if I could talk Mort into hiring me. Maybe Grant wouldn't see me as snooping as I searched for Walter's killer, but only as doing the job of any good reporter: trying to objectively report the truth.

And the truth was, Jasper did not kill his father—I was sure of it. But, I would have to prove it and the best way to do that was to find the person who did.

Yawning, I climbed the stairs back to my bed and Jethro. The chamomile tea and deciding on a course of action at last set my troublesome thoughts to rest. If I had to twist Mort's arm, I would do that. I could hardly wait to go to the newspaper office.

Chapter 18

Fortified by Mom's breakfast of oatmeal, toast, and orange juice, as well as a couple of cups of coffee, I drove to The Ventris Viewpoint, the only newspaper in Levi.

Fog from the Ventris River wound in gray, wispy tendrils like gossamer ribbons around the trees as my car splashed through puddles left from the previous night's rain. I prayed I would not run into a deer. The fog was so thick in places that rounding those blind curves was an occasion for prayer. With relief, I finally drove off the narrow country roads and into Levi where the fog was not as thick.

I had pulled my unruly hair into a twist on the back of my head, and exchanged my blue jeans and T-shirt for tan slacks and a tan-and-red striped, short-sleeved top. Hoping that I looked the part of a serious investigative reporter, I parked in front of the newspaper office and walked inside.

Becky, Mort's young niece and receptionist, looked up with a smile. I told her I'd like to see Mort.

"He's with someone right now, Darcy," she said. "Tell you what—I'm going to the kitchen and we'll pretend I didn't see you. Mort would have my hide if he knew I told you this but if you'll go down the hall and wait outside his door, you'll be able to nab him when his visitor leaves, before he can duck out the back door for his morning coffee at Dilly's." Dilly's was the gathering place for those who wanted the best food in the county. It was an integral part of Levi, and had been since 1946. I loved the old-fashioned décor which had not changed much in seventy years. The home cooking and delicious coffee drew in crowds. It was also the gossip hub of the county and a good place for Mort to pick up news of what was happening.

A few years ago, the dim hallway of the newspaper office would have reeked of cigarette smoke. Today, the tobacco odor was a stale memory, but the hallway still was not well-lighted. I sensed it would have benefited from a serious scrubbing of walls and ceiling.

The stereotype of a hard-bitten newspaper editor who chain smoked and drank coffee all day might have fit Mort except for one thing. Mort did not drink coffee; he drank hot tea.

Hearing loud voices, I paused. Evidently Mort and his visitor had a difference of opinion. Maybe I should go back to the reception area.

"You're a lousy, unscrupulous guttersnipe and I'm warning you, you'd better stop your snooping around before it gets you into serious trouble! Lay off! Do you hear me? Mind your own business or you'll be sorry!"

That loud, agitated voice sounded familiar. I stepped away from the door just in time to keep from being run over by Trace Hughes as he stormed out of Mort's office. His face was as dark as a thundercloud and he strode with long, hurried steps toward the exit. He was so upset, he did not see me in the shadowy hall.

Shocked, I watched the pastor of Levi's Baptist Church stomp toward the outer office. The door slammed before I remembered what I had come for. Hesitantly, I poked my head into the editor's office.

"Mort?" I asked. "Is it safe to come in?"

His gravelly voice tense, he barked, "C'mon on in, Darcy, but only if you don't have a gripe of some kind."

I cleared my throat. "Well, um, no gripe. I was just going to hit you up for a job."

He pushed his swivel chair away from the desk and scowled up at me.

"Sit down. Sit down. I don't feel like getting up and I don't like to talk to a woman who's standing. Puts me at a disadvantage."

Rummaging in his desk, he pulled out a bag of mints and popped one into his mouth.

"Want one?" he asked, offering me the bag. "I've quit smoking, but sometimes I want a cigarette so bad and these things are supposed to help."

I shook my head. His eyes, I noticed, were bloodshot, and his shirt looked as if he had slept in it. Typical Mort. He did not care much about his physical appearance.

Sitting, I decided I might as well be direct.

"What in the world was all that about?" I asked. "You must have done something awful to upset our mild-mannered preacher."

He snorted and his mouth quirked in a sardonic grin. "Mild-mannered? Did that sound mild-mannered to you? I'm telling you, Darcy, your preacher is not what he seems to be. I've been doing some checking. I was curious about why a guy like that, playing and singing like a professional, why he'd come to a little old country town like Levi, and I started digging into his past. I guess he got wind of what I was doin' and didn't appreciate it much. He's not the only one who's pretending. You'd be surprised at how much I know about a lot of people here in Levi."

My heart thudded. "Trace is not what he seems? That's ridiculous! What on earth are you talking about, Mort Bascomb? Have you been listening to gossip?"

"Not gossip, Darcy. I've been investigating a few things I was wonderin' about, and what I heard made me even more curious. I'm going to take a little trip to Georgia, to his hometown. He comes from a small place north of Atlanta called Tyler. I'm that curious. Now what can I do for you? Did you mention a job? If you want to take over my job as editor, you're welcome to it. I'm sick of dealing with irate folk who have something to hide."

"I don't want to be an editor, Mort. I just came to ask if you could use another reporter—me?"

Mort tossed the pencil he had been rolling between his fingers onto his desk where it bounced off a stack of papers and fell onto the floor.

"You're hired," he said.

Chapter 19

"But, Grant, I thought you would be pleased that I have a job to keep me out of trouble."

Grant and I sat in a booth in Dilly's, eating hamburgers and fries, all of it homemade and tasty.

He shook his head. "You and I both know that an investigative reporter hunts up trouble, Darcy. Working for Mort is just an excuse, and don't think you're fooling me, 'cause you're not. Your new job gives you a smoke screen to poke and prod around. I wish you'd let me handle the poking and prodding. Jim and I will find out who murdered poor old Walter Harris, I guarantee it. We are dealing with a killer and whoever he is, he has already killed once. I don't think he'd feel queasy about getting rid of a nosy little reporter who happened to be in his way."

"Thanks for the sermon, Grant. You've never thought I could look after myself."

This conversation had the potential of becoming a spat, something Grant and I had not shared since we were a lot younger. With relief, I saw two familiar figures come through the door. "Look who's here!" I said.

Mom and Jackson Conner edged their way through the lunchtime crowd, back to our booth.

"Do you mind if we join you?" Jackson asked.

Grant nodded. "We'd be honored. Sit down and order. I can vouch for the burgers and fries."

"Darcy, did you get to talk to Mort?" Mom asked as she slid in beside Grant, and Jackson sat next to me.

I swallowed a drink of Coke. "Yes, it looks like I have a job."

Mom shook her head. "I'm not sure how I feel about that. I worried all the time you worked for that Dallas newspaper. Some people don't like a reporter poking into their business."

"That's what I've been telling her," Grant said.

We paused while Jackson gave Tony their order. Chicken fried steak and coffee for these two. They were not fans of burgers and fries.

"I'm sure Darcy will be discreet," Jackson said.

Grant laughed. "Discreet? Are we talking about the same Darcy?"

My face felt hot. It was not pleasant to be talked about, especially when I was present.

"Did you have to twist Mort's arm?" Mom asked.

I dipped a French fry into a puddle of catsup. "Hardly. He was having a bad day and I think he welcomed the idea of a little help."

I told them about overhearing Trace Hughes, and what Mort had said about Trace not being what people thought.

Mom's eyes widened. "You don't mean it. Why, there was never a more polite young man, a better preacher or..."

"Or a better guitarist and singer?" Jackson finished.

"Well, yes," Mom said.

"Just what was Mort talking about?" Grant asked. "He hasn't said a word to me about Hughes. I'm glad to say he has kept his mouth shut as far as publishing anything derogatory about the guy."

Recalling our conversation, I said, "He told me he made some phone calls to a little town in North Georgia, north of Atlanta; Tyler, I believe he said. I don't know who his sources are, Grant. Mort always seems to know things that nobody else knows."

"It's a wonder he hasn't had a lawsuit before now," Jackson said, as Tony brought his and Mom's meals.

We said very little for the next few minutes as we dug into our lunches. Mom and Jackson finished and left, Jackson back to his law office and Mom to check on the progress being made on the new school, Ben's Boys.

Grant and I lingered over our Cokes. Being near him and listening to his deep voice brought back memories of those younger, more carefree days when the whole world was before us, and his place in my heart seemed assured.

"I've bought ten acres from Gil Monroe that joined my ranch on the west," he said. His shy grin reminded me of a little boy, and my heart flip-flopped.

"I'd like you to come and take a look, see if you remember it. It's the prettiest place in Ventris County, on top of a little hill and the Ventris River runs below it."

I couldn't help smiling too at his enthusiasm. "I know the area you're talking about. We explored a cave there when we were just kids. We had heard rumors about some kind of treasure buried inside."

Grant laughed. "It seems to me I recall bats flying out at us which cut our visit short."

Shuddering, I said, "If I have a phobia, it's about bats. Ugh! Something about a flying mammal makes my skin crawl. I've never liked bats! Was that the time we took a picnic lunch down to the river? I'd love to see it again, Grant."

Grant nodded. "Yes, I remember a picnic on the banks of the Ventris River. The river was quiet that day and now, with all the rains, it's muddy and spread out over some of my pasture. But, Darcy, those were happy times. That's one of the reasons I bought it, those old memories. Would after church Sunday be a good time for you to come with me and take a look at it?"

What a romantic gesture! A lot of years had gone between then and now, but he still remembered.

I squeezed his hand. "Perfect."

With that, Grant said he had to get back to the office. Duty called. After he left Dilly's, the bustling café seemed suddenly empty and lonely. I finished my Coke and left too.

Chapter 20

The day after my visit with Mort dawned warm, blue-skied, and still. It was the sort of day when not a breath of a breeze stirred the trees, and the humidity reminded me of a sauna. It was the day of Walter Harris's funeral.

Each time I entered the gates of Goshen Cemetery, memories flooded my mind of the day a year ago last spring when Mom and I came to this sacred place to make sure everything was ready for Decoration Day. What we found here began one of the most terrifying times of my life. This was the final resting place of my dad and many other ancestors, but that awful day last May when we discovered a dead man on top of a pile of brush was the first thing indelibly printed in my memory.

Miss Sugar greeted everyone who came through the cemetery gates. She was the only person I knew whose smile conveyed both sympathy and good cheer at the same time. Miss Sugar's cheerfulness, her roundness, and her white hair reminded me of Mrs. Santa Claus. I could imagine her baking pies and handing Santa cups of hot tea, warning him to keep his coat buttoned and his muffler on. Idly, I wondered if she had met Tim Johnson, the lawn person. They would make a jolly pair.

We walked to the green Shuggart Funeral Home tent spread across a new gravesite. Pitifully few people attended Walter's service. Pat was seated in a chair on the green outdoor carpet spread near the casket poised above a yawning hole in the ground. A single basket of flowers sat nearby. The smell of freshly-turned damp earth permeated the warm air.

"I just don't know what's fitting and proper." Pat had confided to Mom earlier. "It's not as if he was living here as my husband. I never did go to the trouble of getting a divorce so I guess I should attend his service, out of respect for the man I thought he was when I married him years ago."

Mom agreed that if Pat felt this way, she should attend, but should feel no obligation to do so. Walter's long absence had absolved Pat of any burden of responsibility. How could a father just walk away from his child and abdicate his role as mentor and protector? Was Jasper's habit of roaming the woods a result of searching for something to fill the void Walter left?

Pat never did get a divorce? Did she secretly harbor a hope that someday the wandering husband would return? Or did she carry a strong resentment toward the man all these years? This would certainly be understandable. Could Pat have hated him so much she killed him?

My overactive imagination conjured up a worried and wet Pat, searching for her son during a thunderstorm, stumbling upon Walter in Old String's shack, and killing the man who had deserted her and Jasper.

I didn't realize I was staring until Mom nudged me with her elbow.

"Darcy, are you well? You are looking a hole through Pat," she whispered.

With a jolt, I came back to reality and shook my head. How could I suspect Mom's open and honest friend of such a gruesome deed? Mom had known her since they were girls and with Pat, what you saw was what you got. No hidden secrets, no devious thoughts. I was almost sure of that. Almost.

"I just wish Jasper could have been here," Pat said, wringing her hands.

"So do I," Mom murmured. "I wish he could be here to support you."

Mom had told her friend about Jasper's night visit to our house. Knowing her son was safe calmed some of Pat's fears, but she still fretted because he would not come home and let Grant know he had nothing to do with Walter's death.

Burke Hopkins stood alone close to some of the most ancient graves in the cemetery, his arms folded across his chest and his face expressionless. Were some of Burke's ancestors buried here?

Goshen was the final resting place for a woman who had been born before the Revolutionary War. Her grave marker was a strange, four-sided stone. The names of four different people were engraved on it. Goshen Cemetery was a history lesson written in the names of those who had once been a part of Ventris County.

Grant's restless gaze skimmed the cemetery, the woods beyond, and the road which paralleled Goshen. Was he expecting Walter's killer to make an appearance at the funeral? Was he on the lookout for someone lurking among the shadowy trees or driving along the road? Did Grant ever really relax and lay his lawman persona aside?

Besides Miss Sugar and her nephew, we five were the only ones to pay our final respects to Walter.

Pat whispered to Mom, "I don't know where Brother Trace is. He was supposed to say a few words."

"I can't imagine," Mom answered, a frown deepening the lines between her eyes.

Miss Sugar glanced at her watch then spoke to Pat, "I'm sorry your minister isn't here. Would you like us to repeat the Lord's Prayer? Is there anything else you want to add?" With her neatly-ironed handkerchief, Pat dabbed at perspiration beading her face.

"No, no, I can't think of anything. The Lord's Prayer will be fine, Miss Sugar," she said.

So it was that under a hot Oklahoma sun, with ancient pines whispering to each other about strange human rituals and a cardinal singing a cheerful song which belied the solemn occasion, Walter Harris, who came home only to die, was laid to rest.

"Amen," Miss Sugar said, at the conclusion of our recitation. We moved out from under the tent and stood for a few moments while Pat talked with the Shuggarts.

Grant put his hand in the pocket of his jeans.

"Phone call," he explained.

Watching his face as he spoke to the caller, I knew the news was not good. As he returned the phone to his pocket, he glanced down at me, shook his head and sighed.

My heart turned over. "What?" I asked. "What's wrong, Grant?"

Gazing out across the headstones of the ancient cemetery to the far-off pines, the ones that stood in a grove of three trees, Grant spoke softly, almost as if he were talking to himself.

"That was Jim," he said. "He told me some very bad news about Mort Bascomb. Mort is dead."

My ears heard, but my mind was slow to understand.

"Mort? He can't be. I saw him just yesterday, talked to him. He was fine."

Grant replaced his hat and turned on his heel.

"Wait!" I called, hurrying to catch up with him. "Where did he die? When? How did he die? An accident?"

"Stay put, Darcy," Grant snapped, opening the door to his truck. "Let Jim and me handle this."

Chapter 21

Grant had a tendency to be abrupt when he was worried. Mentally, I added that to his list of shortcomings. He was bossy and he was sometimes irritable.

I turned back to Mom and Pat who were walking slowly toward the cemetery gate.

Should I tell them about Mort's death? I hated adding this to Pat's already stressful day and Mom, I knew, would be upset.

"Why did Grant leave in such a hurry?" Mom asked as she and Pat caught up with me.

"He was called to another case," I said. "I'll tell you about it later."

Pat shuddered. "The life of a county sheriff is hard, always having to deal with bad things. Isn't this day awful enough already?"

Mom raised her eyebrows and drew a deep breath.

"Now, Pat" she said, "don't get all worked up again. You've been doing really well. You've closed a sad chapter of your life and you shouldn't look back. Would you like for Darcy and me to go home with you?"

Pat's frown immediately vanished. "Oh, would you? Yes, I'd like that. I really don't want to be alone right now. I baked some cookies yesterday and it won't take a minute to brew a pot of coffee."

"Sure, Miss Pat," I agreed. "To your house it is."

Pat had ridden to the cemetery with the Shuggarts, so we all piled into my Escape and started the short journey to Pat's house in the country. The two friends chatted as I drove. Most of their conversation centered around Trace Hughes and wondering if he had forgotten about the funeral or was ill or what the reason was for his absence. All I could think of was Grant's phone call and the shocking news that the newspaper editor was no longer with us.

When I stopped the car at Pat's, Murphy, the redbone hound who had once belonged to Ben Ventris, got up from his bed on the porch. He plodded down the path to meet us, shaking his head from side to side and voicing a welcome as only a hound can.

After patting Murphy's shiny head and assuring him he was a wonderful animal with an unforgettable voice, I followed Mom and Pat inside her house. Mort Bascomb dead? How? And why? I could not wrap my mind around it. Mort had been as prickly and as well as ever the day before.

"Come on in the kitchen," Pat said, setting her purse beside the door. "It won't take a minute to get us a pot of coffee."

Did the day ever get too warm for coffee? I would have welcomed a glass of iced tea, but maybe Pat needed the comfort of a hot drink after the trauma of the funeral.

We sat at Pat's table drinking coffee, munching sugar cookies and wondering why Trace Hughes was absent from the funeral. Could he have forgotten? Pat did not have his telephone number nor did Mom or I.

Uneasily, I recalled Trace shouting that Mort had better stop snooping or he would get into trouble, that he would be sorry if he didn't stop…stop what? Looking into Trace's background? Did this threat have something to do with his absence today or with Mort's death?

With no warning, Pat started to cry.

Mom got up and came around the table to stand beside her friend.

"There, there," Mom said. "You've had a tough day, but it's over. You can begin a new phase of your life now. Put the past behind you, Pat."

Pat looked up at Mom, her eyes bloodshot and brimming with tears.

"Oh, I know, Flora. I'm not particularly feeling sorry for myself although I could, with all the things that have happened, but I was thinking about Walter and wondering if his eternal soul is with the Lord. You know, he never would go to church with me and when I tried to talk to him about God, he'd always just walk out of the room. I wonder where he is now, Flora. Where is Walter's spirit? Is he with the Lord?"

Mom sighed. "You can't do a thing about that, Pat. Walter is God's concern."

Pat blew her nose and glanced at me.

"Last night, I couldn't sleep, thinking about Walter's funeral today, and all of a sudden, I got the strangest feeling, as if I wasn't alone. Did either of you ever feel that way?"

Thinking back to the old cemetery the night of the housewarming, I nodded.

"Well, anyway, it was a comforting feeling and I think, maybe, Walter might have had time to get right with the Lord just before he breathed his last. Do you all think that's possible?"

"Sure, Pat," Mom said, as I smiled and nodded. "With God, all things are possible."

This seemed to calm Pat. She tucked her handkerchief into her pocket and got up to refill Mom's cup.

I was trying to think of a good way to tell Mom and Pat about Mort when my cell phone jangled. I jumped and sloshed my coffee.

"Sorry," I mumbled, soaking up the mess with a paper napkin. Putting the phone to my ear, I heard Miss Georgia's quavering voice. She didn't ask about ghosts this time.

"Darcy, honey, I'd really like for you and Flora to come right away. Can you, please? I hate to bother you but, well, I just cannot believe what happened out here, on our very own front porch, mind you. It's Mort Bascomb. Have you heard? He's dead. He died right here, Darcy. And Grant thinks we are to blame. I just know he does. Oh, dear."

Soft sobs interrupted Miss Georgia's words. Mort died at the Jenkinses' house? How did that happen? Could this day get any weirder? The nerves tightened in the back of my neck.

"Certainly," I answered. "Take a deep breath, Miss Georgia, please. Drink some calming tea. Mom and I will be there as soon as we can get there."

"No, no," Miss Georgia whispered. "Not tea. That's what got us into trouble."

The sobs had subsided into sniffs before I hung up. Two pairs of anxious eyes stared at me.

"What did Miss Georgia want?" Mom asked. "Is she sick or hurt? What's wrong?"

"We need to go to the Jenkinses' house," I said, placing my soggy napkin inside my cup. "Miss Georgia didn't make a whole lot of sense. She said Grant thinks she and Miss Carolina are to blame for Mort Bascomb's death."

"Mort?" Pat gasped.

"Was that what Grant's phone call was about?" Mom asked. "There must be some mistake. I don't see how he could be dead, Darcy. You just talked to him yesterday. Was it his heart?"

"First Walter, then Mort." Pat shook her head, her tight curls vibrating. "I knew when I heard that owl on my front porch a couple of weeks ago that something was going to happen. I'll bet it was Mort's heart. He used to smoke like a chimney. So, did he keel over at the Jenkinses' house? I don't see how that could be their fault, do you, Flora? Why, I never heard…"

Scooting away from the table as noisily as I could, I carried my cup to the sink. Pat was about to go off on another tirade.

"Actually, I don't know what happened. Grant just said Mort is dead and probably Miss Georgia is imagining Grant blames them for Mort's death. She sounded near hysteria, Mom, so I think we'd better go right now."

"I'll come too," Pat said, starting to get up.

"No, no, Miss Pat." I gently pushed her shoulders down, urging her to stay in the chair. "You've had enough trauma for one day." And, so had I. Dealing with the Jenkins twins would be hard enough, but adding Pat's overwrought nerves to the mix would be too much to handle.

"Come on, Mom, we'd better hurry," I said, taking my mother's hand and hastening toward the door before Pat had time to reconsider.

Mom and I were silent during the drive into Levi. What did Miss Georgia mean when she said Grant blamed them for Mort's death? Why would the Jenkins sisters have anything to do with it? They had never mentioned being friends with Mort. Was he at the Jenkins house trying to nose out information on some story? What happened to the gossipy editor of The Ventris Viewpoint?

Chapter 22

We pulled all the way into the Jenkinses' driveway so that we could enter the house through the back door. This route was faster than running up those steep steps, especially on such a hot day.

Miss Georgia and Miss Carolina, eyes red-rimmed from crying, hugged us and brought us into the parlor.

Mom and I sat beside Miss Georgia on the old-fashioned settee trying to make sense of the twins' disjointed story, which was punctuated by eye-wiping and nose-blowing. Miss Carolina sat across from us in her straight-back wood rocker.

Miss Kitty, knowing that her people were upset, rubbed her head against my arm, jumped up in Miss Georgia's lap, then padded over to Miss Carolina who picked her up and sat absent-mindedly stroking her soft fur.

"I still don't understand why Mort came to see you, Miss Georgia," I said. "You weren't really close friends, were you?"

Miss Carolina answered for Miss Georgia, who was wiping her nose.

"No, that's one of the strange things about this whole ordeal. We'd speak to Mort when we saw him, of course, but goodness me! What would we have in common with a young newspaper editor?"

Young? Maybe to these ladies, who must have been nearing ninety, Mort was young.

"What, exactly, did Mort say?" Mom asked. "Let's start at the very beginning. Tell us Mort's words, as far as you can remember."

"Well...he phoned first and asked if we had a few minutes to spare; he needed to warn us about things he had learned. Isn't that what he said, sister?" Miss Georgia tapped her cheek and stared at the ceiling as if she expected to find something written there.

"Yes, indeed, that's just what he said," Miss Carolina agreed, nodding her snowy white head so vigorously that an old-fashioned plastic hair pin broke loose from its mooring and dangled from the carefully-constructed knot on top of her head. "He wanted to warn us as if we were in danger from something, and that didn't make sense to us."

"And, of course, we said yes he could certainly come and we'd be glad to have him, and it wasn't fifteen minutes later that his car pulled up outside," Miss Georgia added, looking at the grandfather clock as she spoke.

Fidgeting, I wanted to tell them to get on with the story—cut to the chase and tell us what Mort had found that was so important and how did Mort die and where—but I had been raised right. I merely bit my lip and continued stroking Miss Kitty, who had deserted Miss Carolina's lap for mine. Politeness is one of the virtues taught to every Southern child, and I usually tried to be true to Mom's many admonitions about not interrupting my elders, but these ladies were straining the bounds of propriety.

My mother evidently fought the same battle as I and lost. With a short intake of air, she interrupted. "But what did he say? What was so important that he felt he must come in person to tell you?"

"Not *tell*, dear," Miss Georgia said faintly. "A better word would be *warn*. He said he was going to *warn* us...about something."

"But he didn't say what it was?" I prodded.

"It happened this way. You see, we asked if he would like some tea and do you know, he said he would. Most men prefer coffee to hot tea, but that's what he said. So, we were sitting in here, drinking tea."

"And sherry?" I asked.

"That's what caused the problem!" Miss Carolina wailed, as fresh tears slid down her wrinkled cheeks. "That sherry! Now, you know Georgia and I both like just an eensy little tipple in our hot tea but Mort…well, we didn't know he had a drinking problem, but he kept adding more and more sherry until…"

In a rush of words, Miss Georgia finished, "Until Mort's cup held mostly sherry and very little tea." Her eyes widened. "He got drunk, Darcy, not to speak ill of the dead."

This story got stranger by the minute. Gossip had floated around the county for years that Mort sometimes over-imbibed, but I had shrugged it off because no one had ever seen Mort drunk. "Okay, but what did he say that was so important? Why did he feel you needed to be warned?"

"We never found out," Miss Carolina said, mournfully. "Mort was drinking more than he was talking and he kept glancing out of the window and looking around the room as if he expected to see a ghost or something and then…"

"Skittish," Miss Georgia said. "As skittish as Miss Kitty."

Miss Carolina sighed and continued, "And then, all of a sudden, he said that he had been wrong to come and he was going to have to go home. He wasn't feeling so well."

My tense muscles relaxed and I felt as deflated as a limp balloon. All this buildup for nothing? Why on earth had Mort made the trip to the Jenkins house and given them a nebulous warning and then changed his mind? None of this fit together in any logical way.

"But, how did he die?" Mom asked. "Did the alcohol affect his heart? Did he have a stroke?"

Getting up from the settee, Miss Georgia motioned us to follow. She and Miss Carolina led us to the front door.

"He wobbled over here and held on to the door facing," she said. "He really looked pale, and I wanted to phone Dr. McCauley, but Mort was stubborn and said he'd be fine as soon as he was home."

Miss Carolina took up the story. "Then he staggered across the porch and started to go down these very steps. Of course, they are steep. Always have been, and that hand rail has been loose for a while. There's a basement under the house, you know, and you can see a basement window under there and that's why there's so many steps, but Papa put up that hand rail after the house was built. It was Mama, of course. He was so considerate of her. I rather thought a ramp would have been nice, but Papa was opposed to that because it would ruin the symmetry of the house. Mama used the rail to steady herself when she came in the front. Usually, she just walked around the house and came in the back way."

"So Mort made it to the steps, held onto the hand railing and—did he walk to his car?" I asked.

"No, no, dear," Miss Georgia said. "He didn't hold on to the railing. We told him it was easier to go out the back door, but he laughed and said he wasn't an invalid, but as I said, he was pretty wobbly. He lurched against that railing and it came loose. He fell all the way down, Darcy, and he hit his head on that flat rock and he—oh, my goodness! He broke his poor neck!"

Chapter 23

Walking across the porch, I looked down at the ground where the hand railing lay flat, five feet below me. An icy finger of horror traced its way along my spine as I gazed at the spot where a man had died. A picture of Mort flashed through my mind: Mort with his bristly hair, snapping eyes and prickly attitude, fighting against the need for nicotine by popping those mints. At that time neither he nor I could have guessed that only a few hours later he would lie dead beside the stone foundation of the Jenkinses' house.

"Are you all right?" Miss Georgia asked as Mom backed away from the door and leaned against the wall.

"I need to sit down for just a minute," she mumbled, her face as white as the boards of the house.

Concern for my mother dried the twins' tears and brought me immediately to her side. Miss Georgia and I led her to the settee. Miss Carolina disappeared into the kitchen and reappeared with a pot of tea.

Mom rested her head against the back of the settee and closed her eyes. I picked up a magazine and fanned her face.

"I've never fainted in my life and I'm not about to faint now," she said. "I'm feeling better already. Not sure what happened anyway. As I looked out at that porch, I just started feeling sick."

"It was such a shock," I said, accepting the cup Miss Carolina handed me for Mom. "Poor Mort."

For the next few seconds, we four women cried for the newspaper editor who, if not a close friend, was a friendly acquaintance and a fellow human being who did not deserve to have his life cut short.

"Why did you think Grant blamed you?" I asked, blowing my nose and glancing at Miss Georgia.

"Well, he just quite plainly said so," Miss Georgia retorted. "He said if we didn't have that little flask of sherry, Mort wouldn't have gotten so drunk he fell off the porch."

Patting Miss Georgia's hand, I felt a flicker of resentment toward Grant. He should not have further upset these two gentle ladies. On the other hand, what he said was true and I understood his feeling of frustration and grief that Mort's death might not have happened if the twins didn't own that small silver flask.

"I'm all right now, Darcy," Mom said, placing her cup on the coffee table. "The question is, Miss Georgia, are you and Miss Carolina going to be okay? Wouldn't you like to come home with us for a while?"

Smiling, Miss Georgia shook her head. "No, we're fine. We feel better here in our own house, but thank you kindly, dear."

"We'll leave through the back door," I said as Mom and I got up. "However, I'd like to go around front and take a look at that railing. It will need to be repaired right away or maybe you need a new one. Do you think Tim Johnson could repair it? Don't either of you venture out the front until the railing is back up."

"Certainly," Miss Carolina answered.

I walked slowly around those tall steps in the front yard, my eyes on the ground. The sun hung low in the western sky, casting long shadows on the far side of the steps. The broken banister lay as a mute marker of where Mort had lost his life. Kneeling beside it, I lifted it partially off the ground. Surprisingly, it felt heavy. Several screws were gone from the railing which had been used to attach it to the porch. Those screws, rusted and bent, lay on the ground. Why hadn't I insisted that the railing be fixed before this happened? The old railing must have been ready to fall when even the slightest weight rested on it, and Mort had been a big man.

Getting to my feet, I ran my hand over those holes in the side of the house where screws had anchored the railing. Mort's weight against the banister had pulled it completely free of the house's boards.

Sighing, I reached down to help Mom up from the bottom step where she sat. As I glanced at the ground, something glinted in the grass at her feet. Stooping down, I picked up a small, triangular plastic object.

"What is it, Darcy?" Mom asked.

"It's a guitar pick," I said.

"A guitar pick? Why would that be here? Neither Miss Georgia nor Miss Carolina plays a guitar."

A cold, hard knot formed in the pit of my stomach. "Neither did Mort. Do you remember Trace Hughes brought his guitar to our housewarming?"

"Of course," Mom said. "It was a nice gesture and everyone liked hearing him."

"Mort enjoyed the music too. He commented that he had never learned to play anything."

Mom and I were both silent, thinking about what the small plastic object might mean. Trace Hughes played the guitar, the only person of my acquaintance who did. Trace Hughes had threatened Mort the previous day. Trace Hughes did not show up at Walter Harris's funeral.

Mom spoke in a low monotone, her eyes searching my face. "What are you going to do with that pick?"

Bewilderment threatened to overwhelm me as I gazed at the pick in my palm. "I should give it to Grant. It could be evidence. But if it is, Mom, this might mean that Mort's death was not an accident. It could be that someone wanted to make sure Mort didn't tell anybody what he had found out, what he was trying to tell Miss Georgia and Miss Carolina."

My scalp tightened and the hairs on my arms stood up. A strange feeling came over me. Someone, somewhere, was watching us. I gazed around the yard but saw no one. All was quiet. The serenity of the afternoon belied the loss of life which had happened here. Were my nerves so overwrought they were playing tricks on me? Obviously, no one was around, but the cold feeling of dread was real.

Mom shook her head. "I just don't know…" she murmured.

Shaking my head and rubbing my arms, I asked, "Do you have the key to our house here in town?"

She nodded.

"I think it's time we found Mr. Hughes and had a nice, long conversation."

Chapter 24

As I parked in front of our house, my first thought was that the zinnias had recovered nicely since Trace had driven his motorcycle through. That day seemed like such a long time ago.

My mother and I walked up to the familiar porch, climbed the steps, and rapped on the front door. I knocked a second time, more loudly, and a third.

"He isn't home," Mom said.

"Try the key," I said.

But as Mom grasped the doorknob, the door opened. The house had not been locked.

"Reverend Hughes!" I called, stepping inside. "Darcy Campbell and Flora Tucker here."

My voice echoed through the rooms. The kitchen looked bare and unused. I suspected Trace ate most of his meals at Dilly's.

We searched through all the downstairs then climbed to the second floor.

"Trace, are you here?" I yelled, not wanting to embarrass him, or us, by walking in on him if he was in the bathroom or taking a nap.

The upstairs rooms were warm, as if the air conditioner had not been running on this summer day. And although Mom and I knocked on every door, opened them, and looked through the rooms, we found no trace of the pastor of the First Baptist Church of Levi.

In his bedroom, Trace's guitar hung on a stand he had screwed into the wall. Several sheets of manuscript paper lay on his desk. I looked them over. Songs! If Trace was writing a book, as Pat said, it was a book which included some of his original music.

"I don't think he has taken a suitcase or packed any clothes." Mom's voice was muffled inside the master bedroom closet.

"No, it looks as if he just walked out and left his guitar behind," I said. "He's so fond of that guitar, seems to me he wouldn't have left it behind. I didn't see his motorcycle outside, but let's check the garage as we leave."

"And lock the house," Mom said. "We sure don't want some vagrant or whoever murdered poor Walter to walk in and make himself at home."

I sat down on the edge of the bed, propped my elbows on my knees, and rested my chin on my hands.

"Mom, what do we do?" I moaned. "Should I give this guitar pick to Grant? Should I tell him that Trace Hughes is not at home and it doesn't look as if he has been here all day? I just can't believe he would disappear like this without leaving word for anybody."

Mom sat down beside me. "I'm sure there is a good, sound reason he isn't here. Maybe he was called away because of an emergency back home in Georgia. We mustn't jump to conclusions."

Sighing, I stood up. The room was growing dark, and for the first time in my life, the late afternoon shadows in my childhood home seemed menacing.

"Let's go," I said. "Maybe after supper, we'll think of what we should do."

"When we're hungry or worried or don't feel well, we don't make good decisions. Let's eat supper and pray about it. Maybe the Lord will give us some answers."

"Oh, Mom," I said, as we walked into the hallway, "let's hope He does."

As we left, we looked into the garage. Trace's motorcycle was gone. A chill ran down my spine. From the warmth of the house, I'd say he had not been home all day. He forgot about Walter's funeral, and his guitar pick showed up in the Jenkinses' yard. I needed to talk to Trace Hughes. I needed some answers.

Chapter 25

As I drove across our bridge, around the house, and into the garage to park beside Mom's Toyota, a sense of homecoming met me. I loved the trees that seemingly stood guard near our home, the welcoming porch, and the small cat that waited inside the door.

Whippoorwills called from the hollow. Lightning bugs blinked above the grass.

Jethro peered through the glass patio door, impatient to greet us. He meowed a welcome as we stepped inside the kitchen, winding around first Mom's ankles, then mine. Checking his food dish, I saw that it was nearly full. Jethro had his little habits, just as we humans do. Many times he would eat very little or nothing until he was sure that his people were safely home.

Stooping, I ran my hand over his sleek fur. "Have you been a good watch cat?"

"He's probably holding out for a little bit of cream," Mom said. "It won't take long to mix up some cornbread for us, although I don't think Jethro would care for it. Does cornbread and milk sound all right to you for supper?"

"It sounds perfect," I answered.

I set the table, poured milk and placed the butter on the table. Soon the aroma of baking bread filled the kitchen. My stomach growled.

Later, sitting at the dining table and gazing out the patio doors to the woods beyond the garage, which were partially lit by the dusk-to-dawn light, I idly wondered if some of the inhabitants of those woods were looking in at us. What did the 'possums, skunks, raccoons, and rabbits think about us? Did they see us as interlopers in their domain or just fellow creatures whose home looked quite different from theirs?

"What a day," Mom murmured, buttering a piece of warm cornbread.

"Heart-wrenching and exhausting," I answered. "Far too much drama."

"If you want to call it that; anyhow, it was tiring, I agree, and sad."

"Yes, it was sad. I guess it takes a while to actually believe someone is gone when death is so sudden, as Mort's was."

With her finger, Mom traced the beaded moisture on her glass of milk. "Death is such a foreign thing. I don't think I'll ever be able to really believe that your dad is no longer here. Sometimes he seems nearby. I expect to turn around and see those twinkly blue eyes."

My throat felt tight. "Yes. The same is true of Jake. I've heard people talk about 'closure.' To me, that's a meaningless term. So is 'acceptance.' I guess we accept what can't be helped, to a certain extent, but that doesn't mean we have to like it."

Mom's small smile tugged at my heart. "No," she agreed. "We don't have to like it."

Somewhere among the denseness of trees and bushes, an owl hooted. Closer to the house came an answering call. Many times, owls messaging each other was the last thing I heard before drifting off to sleep. Folklore had it that sometimes those calls heralded a rain, but surely another storm wasn't on its way. The grass and herbs were awash in rain.

Wind sighed through the tops of the cottonwood trees in the back yard. Maybe it was because Mort's death lay heavily on my mind that the sound seemed especially mournful tonight.

"Mort said he had been investigating our preacher," I said. "He was curious about why a man with as much talent as Trace would come to a small town like Levi."

"Maybe he felt the Lord led him," Mom said. "He seems to be such a sincere young man. It could be that he is satisfied using his music for the Lord."

"I hope that's right. Mort said that Trace comes from a small town in north Georgia, Tyler. How would you feel about paying a visit to Tyler, Georgia?"

Mom dropped her cornbread and stared at me.

"Darcy Tucker Campbell! Are you serious?"

I nodded. "Mort mentioned Trace's hometown, and I think he was planning on making a trip to visit there. Mort did hire me, so I guess I am officially working for his newspaper. However, I want to do this for myself. I think Trace Hughes did not tell us everything. I want to find out exactly why he is here…somewhere. Or maybe I'm too late. Maybe he has left town. Tomorrow I'll call for airplane reservations to Atlanta. Want to come?"

Mom fidgeted. "You know how I feel about flying. I think if the Lord had meant us to fly like birds—"

"I know, he would have given us wings. Well, he did, sort of. Only the wings are on an airplane. It's all right if you don't go, Mom. In fact, you probably should stay here to see if anything develops about Mort's death and if Trace shows up again."

"You've convinced me," Mom said. "Only thing is, I wish you didn't think it was important enough to make that long trip."

"I'll call you if it's necessary to be there more than a day. Please stay safe, and be sure to call Grant if you feel threatened in any way."

"How soon are you leaving?" Mom asked.

"Hopefully, tomorrow. I'll call and see if I can get a flight out of Fayetteville."

Chapter 26

The flight from Fayetteville, Arkansas, took less than two hours. It was just after noon when the plane landed in Atlanta. As soon as I could do so after arriving, I rented a car, and followed a map northward toward Tyler.

The narrow, two-lane road curved up and around mountains thickly clothed with tall trees, many of them pines. This was the home of my ancestors, my mother's people. It was also in the vicinity of Dahlonegah, Georgia, the "place of the yellow" where gold was discovered. That discovery resulted in the infamous Trail of Tears when the Cherokee people were forcibly removed from their homes and driven west to Indian Territory. I could not think of that sad episode without a heavy feeling on my heart.

Catching a glimpse of brown out my side window, I braked just in time to keep from hitting a deer which, heedless of the danger, leapt on springy hooves across the highway in front of me. As I was taking a deep breath to steady my nerves, another deer followed and yet another. Evidently, these deer traveled in families, or maybe the rest of the clan watched to see whether the lead deer crossed safely.

A half mile past the deer crossing, I saw a small wood sign. TYLER in bold, black letters stood out from the painted wood. A narrow, paved lane branched off to the right. If I hadn't slowed for the deer, I might have zipped right past that sign and not known it was there.

Five miles along this road brought me to a small, pretty settlement. The road I traveled became the main street of Tyler. On one side of the street sat a grocery store, not a chain store, but one with a large window in front on which the words TYLER GROCERY blazed forth.

On the other side of the grocery store was a post office, a gas station, and a library. The library sat back from the street and was prettily landscaped with rose bushes and dogwood trees and a fountain, under which some robins and cardinals were enjoying a bath.

Past the library on the opposite side of the street, a small, neat sign proclaimed BAPTIST CHURCH OF TYLER. Several other streets nestled near the church which seemed to be in the center of Tyler. The white wood building reminded me of the church at home with its spire and bell. A neat-looking house, which I supposed was the parsonage, stood beside the church. Thick pine woods began directly behind the church, as if the forest only grudgingly gave way to civilization.

This seemed a logical place to begin my search, since I was inquiring about a preacher. Stopping the car in the gravel parking lot, I climbed out and walked to the double front door.

Knocking got no response, so I tried opening the door. Locked! Why would a house of worship in such a small town need to lock its doors? Shouldn't it be a sanctuary for people wanting to go inside and pray any time of the day or night?

Now what? Undecided, I meandered toward my car.

"Mebbe you're lost?"

Whipping around, I tripped over my own feet.

A wrinkled, bent man with thinning white hair, a beak nose and piercing brown eyes under bushy brows stood within three feet of me.

For a few seconds, I stared at him, waiting for my heart to get out of my throat and flip back to its usual place beneath my ribs. Where had he come from? Was this a gnome who materialized from behind a tree?

"No, I'm not lost," I croaked. "I'm looking for somebody."

"Well, speak up, young 'un. Who you lookin' for?"

Swallowing, I struggled to gather my thoughts. "I'm…uh…I'm looking for Trace Hughes, actually. I heard this is his hometown."

"Preacher Hughes?"

I nodded.

Shaking his head, the old man mumbled, "You're just a mite too late. Pastor Hughes died. That he did. We ain't got no preacher no more. Had to lock up the church building. Sad, sad."

"No." I shook my head. Trace could not be dead. He was young and vibrant and alive. The day grew cold and I shuddered with a sudden chill.

"This can't be true."

The wrinkled gnome of a man nodded. "'Fraid it is, hard as it is to hear it."

Licking my dry lips, I took a deep breath. "He's dead? Are you sure? How did it happen? It must have been recent."

"Rutherford Galway, what are you telling this young woman?"

A tall, thin, gray-haired woman strode toward me from the direction of the small house next to the church.

"She was askin' about Pastor Hughes," Mr. Galway said, jerking a thumb toward me.

The newcomer's eyes, as sharp as ax blades, squinted at me for a few seconds. Pursing her lips, she said, "I see. Have you come a long way?"

"I live in Levi, Oklahoma. I just flew in to Atlanta today. My name is Darcy Campbell."

Forcing a smile, I stepped toward her, holding out my hand.

"Gladys McEvers," she said. Her handshake was firm.

"Why are you looking for Pastor Hughes?" Gladys McEvers's voice was as crisp and cool as her handshake.

"I've got some questions and thought the answers might lie here." A splitting headache threatened to crack my skull wide open. "Trace Hughes is our preacher at the Baptist church in Levi, Oklahoma. I understand he is from Tyler. You see, he disappeared. I thought maybe I could find some answers in his hometown. But, Mr. Galway said he is dead. I don't understand."

I glanced toward Rutherford Galway but he had disappeared.

"Where did he go?" I stammered, glancing at trees and bushes to catch a glimpse of him.

"Pay him no nevermind," Gladys said, waving her hand as if she were batting at mosquitoes. "He comes; he goes. He likes to slip around as silent as a mouse. You look tired and a mite poorly. Why don't you come into the house for a glass of tea? I think we need to talk."

Chapter 27

I swallowed a long drink of iced tea and glanced around this clean, sunny living room. It was comfortably furnished with a brown leather sofa and matching chair, two cushy recliners, lots of books in shelves, and a small fireplace.

Glancing at the fireplace mantel, I did a double take. Several pictures sat there, family pictures, I assumed. One was of an attractive young man and a teenage girl, the other was the same two people with an older man. The younger man was my preacher, Trace Hughes.

Gladys McEvers smiled. "You recognize Pastor Hughes?"

"Of course. The young lady resembles him. His sister?"

Setting her glass of tea on the vinyl floor so quickly that some of it sloshed out, Gladys jumped from her chair and trotted to the fireplace. She pointed to the picture of Trace and the young woman.

"Is this who you are calling Pastor Hughes?"

Now it was my turn to be flabbergasted. "Why, yes."

Pressing her hand over her mouth, Gladys shook her head. "I've got to sit down," she said.

This was strange behavior but I waited quietly, sensing that Gladys would speak when she was able to collect her wits. She seemed completely bewildered.

My hostess was silent for so long, I grew impatient.

"I'm sorry, Miss McEvers, I'm not understanding. Do you mean that man is not Pastor Hughes?"

Gladys shook her head and clasped her hands together. She spoke so softly, I leaned forward to hear her.

"No, he's not. He is Trace Hughes, Jr., our pastor's son. The girl is his younger sister, Melanie."

I felt as if my breath had been knocked out of me. What was going on?

"Let's share stories," Gladys said, her voice stronger. "I sort of look after the church and the parsonage, keep everything spic and span, you know. I've done that since Pastor Hughes died and Melanie left home."

"So, it was the elder Hughes who was your minister? He is the one who died, and not his son?"

Gladys nodded.

I should not have felt such relief, because death is death, but a weight lifted from my heart. Trace was still among the living.

"When did he die? And why did Melanie leave home? Did Trace live here too? Why did he tell the church in Levi he is a preacher if he isn't? Or did he pastor a different church?"

Wearily, Gladys shook her head. "It's a sad story and one that hasn't ended yet. Not really. You see, Pastor Hughes was a mighty good preacher but strict, kind of hard on his kids, seemed to me, wouldn't allow them to be less than perfect. Maybe he felt the responsibility of bringing them up by himself. Mrs. Hughes died a few years back. Anyway, Melanie was a good girl, a pretty girl as you can see, but she rebelled against her father's stern rules and she...well, she got pregnant."

"And she wasn't married," I guessed.

"No, not married and it about killed her father. He told her to leave and not come back, that she had disgraced her family. So, that's what she did. She left and nobody knew where she went exactly."

"What do you mean 'exactly'? Did somebody know her whereabouts?"

Gladys frowned and waggled her index finger.

"Now, just a minute, Miss Campbell, I'm coming to that. After Melanie left, Pastor Hughes saw that he had been too harsh. He was sorry he threw her out, worried what might happen to her. Well, he grieved himself into a heart attack. Yes, sir. That's what he did."

The wind sighed through the pines and a cloud passed across the sun, throwing the living room into shadows.

"I'm so sorry," I said. "But why did Trace wind up in Levi, Oklahoma? Where does he fit in with all this? Is he a preacher or isn't he? I can't believe he lied to the church back in Levi."

Going to the bookcase, Gladys opened a drawer and pulled out a magazine. She handed it to me.

The name on the cover of the magazine was *Musician's Scene*. The cover of this slick magazine featured a younger Trace Hughes, a smiling Trace with a guitar in his hands.

Quickly thumbing pages, I skimmed the articles.

"It looks like Trace was a well-known musician, at least throughout the South. He has made some best-selling records," I murmured. "No wonder he sounds like a professional musician. He *is* a professional."

Gladys sat down, crossed her legs, and leaned toward me.

"When he heard that Melanie left, Trace came back home. He and his dad had words. He was so upset when he talked to me! I felt sorry for him. You see, he had always been close to Melanie and he blamed his dad for her predicament, said his dad had no understanding of a young girl. Then he said somebody, one of his buddies, heard she was hitchhiking, trying to get to a friend out in California and she had made it as far as a little place in northeast Oklahoma."

"Levi," I whispered.

"Yes, well, maybe. He didn't say. But when Pastor Hughes died, Trace wrote to me and asked me to keep lookin' after this place. He didn't even come back for Brother Hughes's funeral, but he sent a wad of money. As if I needed pay for doing what's my boundin' Christian duty. Anyhow, that's all I know about this awful situation."

"Thank you, Miss McEvers," I said as I placed my empty glass on the floor and stood up.

Gladys rose too.

"Oh, please, you don't have to go. You can't mean that you are going all the way back to Oklahoma tonight? The parsonage has a guest room, bed freshly made up. You're welcome to stay and then get an early start home tomorrow."

The truth was, I could not wait to be on that plane, soaring through the sky to Levi. I would just have time to make the evening flight back to Fayetteville where I had left my Escape. My trip to Tyler had netted shocking news, but I couldn't see that this explained the mystery of Trace's disappearance from Levi. As for Trace himself, he was not here. Where was he? Trace, his father, Melanie…all gone. Tyler was a sad place.

Chapter 28

"I just can't believe it," Mom said for the fourth time, turning her coffee cup around and around in its saucer. "Our pastor is a fraud? Can you believe it, Darcy?"

Wearily shaking my head, I sighed. "It is a hard thing to wrap my mind around, but it's pretty clear. He let us believe a lie, that he was the elder Trace Hughes. I suppose his motive was good, though. He must have thought if he gave us a reason to be here, he would have ample time to search for Melanie. And there was the letter from our church to his father. We didn't know his father had died, of course."

"You must be worn out. It's after midnight. Why don't you go to bed and maybe things will look better with the sunrise."

"I couldn't sleep, Mom. As I flew back from Atlanta, I'll bet I rehashed Gladys's and my conversation a dozen times. By the way, do you have any aspirins in the cabinet?"

"Third shelf to the left of the sink," Mom answered.

Lightning flickered across the horizon as I glanced out of the kitchen window. I rinsed my cup in the sink and reached up for the aspirin bottle.

"Looks like another storm coming. I once liked rain, but this summer I'm growing mighty tired of it."

"I think that's just heat lightning," Mom said.

An owl hooted down in the hollow and another answered, the age-old omen for a coming storm.

"Or maybe not," she added.

Jethro rubbed against my ankles. Scooping him up, I returned to the table. Stroking his silky head helped my racing thoughts to slow.

Upstairs by my computer sat an incomplete manuscript. After I had finished the book about folk tales and legends of Ventris County, my publisher asked for a sequel. This book, however, was coming along slowly. Life kept getting in my way. Rain was a pleasant accompaniment to writing. Perhaps tomorrow I could finish another chapter.

"What do you think about all this?" I asked my cat. He squeezed shut his eyes and seemed to consider.

"Do you honestly think that Trace had a hand in Mort's death?" Mom asked.

"The evidence, such as it is, is purely circumstantial," I said, imagining that Jethro's loud purring meant he agreed with that statement. "Let's look at this, Mom. I heard Trace more or less threaten Mort. Trace wasn't at Walter's funeral, a sad omission for a pastor. And then, Mort turned up dead and I found the guitar pick by the Jenkinses' front porch. That doesn't prove a thing, but it does cast doubt. Mort had planned to go to Tyler. Maybe Trace didn't want him to go for fear of what Mort might find out."

Mom raised her eyebrows. "Of course he wanted to keep his real identity a secret, but surely not to the extent of silencing Mort. He pretended to be someone he wasn't. I can't think that he had anything to do with Mort's death, but why did he disappear if he hadn't?"

Wishing the aspirin would hurry and ease my pounding head, I said, "Levi is full of disappearing people. I don't suppose Jasper has come home?"

"No. I talked to Pat a few hours ago and she was still wishing he would show up. She's afraid Grant will think he had something to do with Mort's death as well as Walter's."

"That's just silly. But, knowing Pat, she does have a tendency to jump to conclusions without benefit of anything factual."

Wrinkling her nose at the taste, Mom drained the last of her cold coffee. "Ugh! I've had enough coffee for ten people. I've been worrying about something. Surely, Trace is not tied in somehow with Walter's death? Do you think?"

"I don't see how or why. He may not really be a preacher, and he may have taken advantage of the invitation his father got from our church, but murder? Oh, my goodness, Mom, I cannot believe that he would kill anyone."

"I've always thought I'm a pretty good judge of character," she said as she carried her cup to the counter and returned to the table. "He has an honest face."

Jethro jumped to the floor and I dusted off my jeans. "Maybe you should look for other evidence of character," I said. "He certainly is not ordained to preach. He's a professional singer."

My mother fidgeted, looking down at her place mat. "He didn't actually lie. His name really is Trace Hughes. We just thought he was the elder, and he didn't tell us any different. And, he can sure sing those hymns."

Grinning, I reached over and patted her hand.

"Oh, Mom, when you like someone, you find all kinds of excuses for them, don't you?"

She sniffed. "I'm not excusing what he has done at all, Darcy, but I just have to believe that young man loves the Lord. He sings and speaks likes he really means those words."

"You know," I interrupted, "I believe I can sleep now, if I can make it up to bed."

The stress of the past few days caught up with me in a rush. My eyelids felt as if they weighed a ton. I shuffled toward the stairs. Everything could wait until morning.

"By the way," Mom called as my hand touched the newel post, "Miss Carolina said more food has disappeared."

"Sure, why not?" I muttered. "Disappearing people, disappearing food, there must be a reason for all this but right now, I'm too tired to think about it."

Chapter 29

The owls last night proved to be good weather predictors. Rain ran in gray sheets down the windows in the sheriff's office where I sat. However, instead of spending the day at my computer adding to my book, I had chosen to talk to Grant. There were some things we needed to discuss.

Grant held the guitar pick between his thumb and forefinger and gazed at it as if it were a carrier of bubonic plague.

"So you found this outside the Jenkinses' house and you didn't say anything to me about it?" he asked, leaning back in his chair and never taking his eyes off the pick.

I bit my lip. "Well, no, I didn't know what to do. I don't know how it got there, but I'm sure it has no bearing on Mort's death."

"No, of course not. Probably Miss Georgia dropped it on her way to play guitar at the old folks' home," he sneered.

Heat flared across my face.

"Now, listen, Grant Hendley, if I had wanted to protect Trace Hughes, I would never have shown you that guitar pick at all. I would have thrown it away."

"Okay. Sorry, Darcy. I'm a little on edge. So, you went to Tyler, Georgia? Why?"

How much should I tell Grant? Mentally shrugging my shoulders, I decided to include everything I had learned. In a way, it might help to absolve Trace of suspicion. He was, after all, on a charitable mission to find his young sister. Surely that showed compassion and would explain that he was in Levi for a good reason, not a nefarious one.

As I finished my story, Grant dropped the guitar pick on his desk, ran his hands through his red hair and glowered at me.

"Are you sure he didn't drop it when he went to visit with the Jenkins ladies?"

"They said he had never visited them. They go to the Methodist church, you know. I think the only time they saw him was at our housewarming."

"Darcy, this guy is a fake and a liar. I mean, it's bad enough to pretend to be someone he's not, but to pretend to be a preacher!"

"Are you going to get prints off that guitar pick?" I asked, hoping to divert Grant from the obvious shortcomings in Trace's character.

"I can have it dusted and compare the prints to those in your rent house, but how would that prove anything we don't already know?"

"You mean that we 'suspect', Grant. We don't *know* anything for sure."

"I know I never trusted Trace Hughes from the first. He has conveniently disappeared, so I can't question him. He didn't show up for Walter's funeral, threatened Mort and Mort's dead. I went back to the Jenkins house and had another look at that railing and the steps. Those screws holding the banister to the porch could easily have been removed, maybe just one left in to keep it in place."

"But, Grant, Trace would not have known Mort was going to the Jenkins home. Miss Georgia or Miss Carolina could have walked down those steps."

Grant shook his head. "You're right. The only way this theory would work would be if Hughes was watching the house or trailing Mort and when he saw Mort go inside, he slipped over and removed some screws."

I remembered the sense I had of being watched when Mom and I were last at the Jenkins house. But, it was only a feeling, nothing I wanted to mention to Grant.

Standing up, I said, "That sounds pretty unlikely. I think you're providing a scenario for a conclusion you've already reached. You're hunting for facts to support your belief that Trace is guilty. Next, you'll be telling me that Trace and Jasper are accomplices and are hiding out somewhere together."

"You look cute when you get mad, you know." Coming around his desk, he took my hand. "I don't want you to be mad, though. How about going out and taking a look at my new ten acres I told you about?"

"It's raining," I protested, but I did not withdraw my hand.

"If we do anything this summer, looks like it's going to have to be in the rain. Let's go by Dilly's and get a couple of hamburgers. It won't exactly be a picnic like last time, but at least you can see what I have in mind. I want to expand my ranch, maybe build a bigger house on top of that hill. What do you say?"

Looking into Grant's blue eyes, I saw the pleading there. This meant a lot to him. I would go, rain or no rain.

"All right," I said. "You've convinced me."

Chapter 30

Grant and I sat in his truck, munching our burgers, our cups of coffee steaming up the windows in the cab. Listening to the rain, looking out at the green countryside, and hearing Grant tell me about his plans for his ranch gave me a warm, contented glow. There was nowhere else I would rather be.

We were parked above the cave we had explored as children. The Ventris River rolled below us, muddy and spread out from the rain.

"You will have to build your house as far as you can from the river," I said. "It would be awful if you were flooded."

He nodded. "What I had in mind was a log house, not nearly as large as yours and Miss Flora's, but large enough for two people, just to start with. I'd like a fireplace, maybe two bedrooms, a kitchen and a bath."

I didn't ask who he had in mind to share it with him. This was a serious subject and I had a way of sounding flippant at times.

"And a nice, wide front porch," I chimed in, catching his enthusiasm.

He grinned. "Sure. I like porches."

"Oh, Grant, that sounds perfect!" I said. "I can see it all now."

And, I could. I could even envision sitting on the porch with Grant, watching the sunsets. Images of Jake were coming to my mind less and less frequently, but I needed to be honest with Grant. I was not sure I was ready to consider a second marriage.

Grant took my hand. "The only thing I need to make it perfect is…"

He stopped and stared out of the side window.

"What?" I asked. "What is it, Grant?"

"A truck," he said. "I just caught a glimpse of it going over the hill. Somebody is trespassing. If he left the gate open in the south pasture, the cattle will get out. I'm going to drive down a little farther."

Starting the engine, Grant drove quickly down the hill toward the cave.

"I'm going to get out and take a look around," he said.

"Wait. You'll need an umbrella. I'm going with you."

We left his truck, ducked under my umbrella, and walked toward the mouth of the cave. Tire tracks showed plainly in bent-over grass. In the distance, I heard a motor growing fainter.

"What would somebody be doing out here on such a day?" I wondered.

Grant shook his head. "I didn't see the truck well enough to identify it. Did you?"

"I didn't see it at all," I answered. "Maybe some sightseer just wanted a look at the flooded river."

"Could be," Grant said. "Come on, let's drive over and check the gate, then I'll take you back to town."

The romantic, warm mood was definitely over. I wasn't sure if I was disappointed or relieved.

Sure enough, the pasture gate was wide open. Muttering about trespassers, Grant drove through the gate, got out and closed it, then followed the lane to get back on the main road to Levi.

When I got home, I found Mom, not serenely drinking coffee, but pacing the floor and wringing her hands.

"Oh, Darcy," she said as I opened the door from the back porch into the kitchen. "I'm so glad you are home. Hiram called and said he thinks somebody has been digging where the old cellar was at Ben's farm. He said he's been seeing lights out there at night, but when he went to investigate, he couldn't find anybody."

"Whoa, wait a minute, Mom. Slow down. Hiram Schuster called you?"

Putting my arm around her, I guided her to a kitchen chair.

"Yes, Hiram! You know he's putting the finishing touches on Ben's Boys and it'll be ready to open this fall. He's been staying in the main house at night, trying to catch whoever is digging. He said whoever it is has made a trench about two feet deep on top of that mound of dirt and rocks that was once the cellar."

Going to the stove, I turned on a burner and scooted a kettle of water over the flame.

"I'm going to make you a cup of chamomile tea, Mom. You are entirely too worked up. So, who does Hiram think it is, and why is he calling you now?"

"For goodness sake, Darcy, he's calling because he wants me to know about it! It has been so rainy this summer that the ground is soft and easy to dig, and who knows how far this person is going to go? Maybe there's an air shaft or something and he will find his way into the cellar and—"

"You are borrowing trouble, Mom. We don't know why this person is digging, whether he knows something about what's under there or if he's looking for Indian arrowheads or what. Whatever his motive, though, he's got to know that he is trespassing, at the very least."

"It may be a good idea to tell Grant. Maybe he or Jim could stake it out some night and catch whoever it is."

Maybe. Maybe not. Grant would give me a lecture about not getting involved with trespassers and, after our closeness today, I hated to bring up a subject that might do anything to change that.

Putting some dried chamomile into a diffuser, I placed it in a cup, covered it with hot water and gazed through the window at the summer storm. If anybody got out in weather like this, he had to be very determined.

Adding a dollop of honey to the tea, I carried the cup to Mom and sat down across from her at the dining table.

"Thank you, Darcy," Mom said, cradling the cup between her palms. "It must be this damp weather that makes me feel cold. I'm getting to be really tired of all this rain!"

"I know," I said. "Missing people don't help our moods either. And two deaths."

We were both silent, listening to the rain drumming on the porch.

"As soon as the rain lets up, do you want to go out to the school and take a look?" I asked.

Mom nodded. "Maybe we should stop by the Jenkins house first and find out about more food missing. Isn't this a tangle?"

"Indeed," I agreed. "'Through many dangers, toils, and tangles, I have already come,'" I sang, changing slightly the words to "Amazing Grace."

She shook her head at me and a ghost of a smile flitted across her face. This was the effect I had hoped for.

"Darcy! Stop that! That's almost sacrilegious."

"Sorry. Let's get into our rain jackets and go to the Jenkinses," I said. "Rain or not, we can certainly talk to Miss Georgia and Miss Carolina then go on out to the school, if the rain lets up."

Chapter 31

The rain stopped before we got to the Jenkins home. The sun came out, gilding every leaf with a washed-clean glow.

I parked in the Jenkinses' driveway. Tim Johnson, a toolbox in his hands, was kneeling beside the porch step's railing. He turned to us with a grin spreading across his ruddy face.

"There!" he said. "Good as new. Maybe better. I'll bet that old railing had been near to coming down for a long time."

"Thanks," I said. "Mom and I will be the first ones to test your handiwork. I gave strict orders to the twins that they were to use the back door until this railing was fixed."

Tim shook his head. "Sure wish I had nailed it back before that poor fellow fell to his death. Makes me feel responsible somehow."

"Nonsense! I've been meaning to tell you how much I appreciate your mowing the grass at our house. You are a much better mower than I am."

Nodding his thanks, Tim Johnson carried his toolbox to his truck. We went up those steep front steps and knocked on the Jenkinses' door.

Miss Georgia and Miss Carolina always hugged us when they saw us, even if that happened to be twice in the same day. Surprisingly, this time they did not offer us hot tea but the iced variety served in tall, frosted glasses, with sprigs of mint atop the ice.

Grave Heritage

Miss Georgia shook her head.

"We've gotten rid of that troublesome flask," she said. "I just didn't realize it would ever cause someone to fall to his death."

Mom squeezed her hand. "Don't be too hard on yourselves," she said. "Are you certain that more food disappeared?"

"Oh, yes," said Miss Carolina. "This time, it was a loaf of bread, some peanut butter, and a quart of milk."

Lifting the mint from off a floating cube of ice, I crunched it and eyed Miss Carolina.

"Have you seen any more flitting people in white?"

Looking down at her folded hands, she shook her head. "No. Nary a one. No more ghosts or anything."

"We haven't even smelled Papa's pipe lately," Miss Georgia said. "I guess that's a good sign."

A niggling suspicion was just below the surface of my consciousness. Could it be possible that the missing food and missing people were somehow connected?

"Mom, didn't you think it odd when Jasper didn't eat all the food you fixed for him but took about half of it with him?"

"Yes, it was certainly strange," Mom mused. "I've never known anybody with a larger appetite than Jasper. When he was a lot younger and came to Vacation Bible School, why, at snack time, it was almost impossible to fill that boy up."

So, it seemed that Jasper had always had a hollow tooth or leg. My mother's patience with Pat's son never failed to amaze me.

"I wonder if anything over at Miss Pat's has gone missing. Besides Jasper, I mean."

Mom snapped her fingers. "The other day, she said she couldn't find a quilt that her grandmother made a long time ago. I put it down to Pat's forgetfulness. With Walter's death and Jasper's disappearance, it's a wonder she doesn't forget her own name."

Miss Carolina raised her eyebrows and glanced at Miss Georgia, who shrugged and looked bewildered.

I realized that the twins probably did not know a lot about recent goings-on, other than the strange happenings here in their own home.

"I'm sorry," I said. "Pat's son Jasper has been hiding out since his father's death, but he came to our house the other night and conned us out of some food."

"Oh, my," Miss Georgia whispered. "The poor boy. All he'd have to do is ask and we'd give him all the food he wanted."

Mom frowned. "Darcy! He didn't con us out of anything. He asked for food and I gave him food."

"Did you tell Grant?" asked Miss Carolina.

"Not yet," I said, "so please don't breathe a word to anybody else."

Miss Carolina giggled. "I love secrets."

"If he's hungry, why doesn't he just go home? I doubt that his mother would turn him in to the sheriff," Miss Georgia said.

Mom set her empty glass on the tray on the coffee table. "Jasper is the most secretive young man I've ever seen. He enjoys knowing things that nobody else knows. He knew where Ben Ventris was a long time before we finally found him. He's more at home in the woods and with the animals than he is with people."

"Help me out with this," I said. "Melanie, Trace Hughes's sister, was last seen in this area of Oklahoma, according to the woman in Tyler. Right?"

Mom nodded and the sisters shrugged.

Talking slowly, I tried to put my suspicions into words. "Jasper likes to help people or animals he thinks are needy. Jasper is in hiding because he's afraid Grant will look on him as a suspect in Walter's death."

"And Jasper could never bear being locked up," Mom interjected.

Standing, I bent to pick up the tray of empty glasses. "Two things about Jasper's character are his love of being secretive and his compassion for animals and birds. He sympathizes with anything or anybody needing protection. Melanie may be hiding because she doesn't want to be sent back home. She's young and scared and certainly would qualify for Jasper's sympathy," I said. "And the disappearing food could be going to Melanie."

Mom gasped. "You don't mean it!" she said.

"Do you mean our missing food?" Miss Georgia asked.

"It's just a thought," I said.

Carrying the tray to the kitchen, I set it in the sink. Something about this kitchen was not right. Something was different, but what? I turned full circle, peering at the old-fashioned stove, the polished oak table and chairs, and the china cabinet full of fragile antique cups and teapots. As I glanced at the pantry and cellar doors, my heart skipped a beat then thudded.

That was it! Someone had tampered with the cellar door.

Going back to the living room, I put my finger to my lips and said in a loud whisper, "Come into the kitchen, but come quietly. I want to show you something."

The Jenkins twins tottered after me, their eyes wide. Mom trotted along behind them.

"What in the world is wrong, Darcy?" she asked.

I pointed to the cellar door. The deadbolt which I thought had been rusted shut was slid back. The door was no longer locked.

The three women gasped.

"What does it mean?" Miss Carolina whispered. "We haven't unlocked that door for years."

Mom patted her arm. "I think it means someone has been using your cellar."

I looked around at the three wide-eyed women. "And that someone may be down there right now."

"Oh, no," Miss Georgia moaned. "Call Grant. Quick."

"No, no. Wait. I don't think whoever is down there is dangerous."

"How on earth could you possibly know that, Darcy?" Mom asked. "Lock the door again and call Grant."

Giving my cell phone to Mom, I said, "If I yell, hit Grant's number. Miss Georgia, do you have a flashlight?"

"Certainly, Darcy honey, but I really don't think…" began Miss Georgia.

"Here it is, Darcy," Miss Carolina interrupted. "Now, be careful. Those old steps are rickety."

"I'll say a prayer for you," whispered Miss Georgia.

I smiled at her, eased the cellar door open, and shone the light into the darkness below me. One by one, I descended the steps until I reached the stone floor of the basement. Beaming the light around the dark space, I spotted a huddled shape in one corner. The shape moved and whimpered.

"Please, I'm sorry for trespassing," said a feminine voice.

A young woman, wrapped in a quilt, sat against the cellar wall. My light shone on long, dark hair, a white face, and large, frightened eyes.

"Don't be scared," I said softly, going to her and offering my hand. "I'm Darcy Campbell and you are in my grandmother's house. I believe I know who you are. Come on up and meet the rest of us."

Chapter 32

Melanie Hughes sat at the Jenkins dining table, clutching Pat's quilt around her shoulders, shaking. She looked much the same as the photograph I had seen in Tyler, only more like a scared child instead of the confident teenager in the picture.

Miss Georgia brought out her seldom-used coffee pot, and soon each of us cradled a warm cup. We tried not to stare at the young, frightened girl sitting with us.

I waited until she had finished half of her coffee before voicing what was uppermost in my mind.

"How long have you been in that basement?" I asked.

"I don't know. Maybe a week. Jasper thought it was probably a week," she said, her teeth chattering.

"Jasper?" Mom asked. "Has Jasper been helping you?"

A shaky smile lit her face. "Oh, yes. I don't know what I would have done without Jasper. He brought food, this quilt."

Miss Carolina shook her head. "To think you've been right here in our house and we didn't know it. Why didn't you just knock on our door? Why hide out in that cold basement? Why, it's a wonder you didn't catch your death."

"I noticed a few pieces of furniture down there," I said. "Did Jasper, by chance, find them in the carriage house?"

"Yes, he did," Melanie said, swallowing more coffee. "I'm sorry about using them. It wasn't exactly stealing, you know."

Slipping around the table, Miss Kitty ignored all our laps until she got to Melanie. Leaping up, she snuggled against Melanie, who automatically dropped a hand onto the old cat's head. So, Miss Kitty probably had known Melanie's whereabouts all this time and became acquainted with her while the twins were asleep or out of the house.

A thumping below us jerked our heads in the direction of the basement. Footsteps thundered up the steps and the door beside the pantry banged open. Jasper, wild-eyed and disheveled, stood in the kitchen glaring at us.

"Why don't you just let her alone?" he bellowed. "She ain't done nothin' wrong. She's scared, can't you see that?"

Mom went to Jasper and put her hand on his arm.

"Of course we see, Jasper, and you have been helping her the best you knew how. You came through the window downstairs, didn't you? Come sit down and I'll pour you a cup of coffee."

Between Jasper and Melanie, we soon heard her pitiful story. Yes, she had run away from home, and she had not heard about her father's death. Nor did she know her brother was in Levi, hunting for her. She was at the end of her small horde of money and not feeling well when she reached town. Jasper found her in the Jenkinses' carriage house, but he was afraid she would be discovered there. He suggested the basement and tried to fix it up to be comfortable for her.

"But why did you feel you had to hide?" Miss Georgia asked. "Why didn't you just tell us your story? You could have stayed right here in a room upstairs instead of stuck away in that musty old basement."

A tear slid out of the corner of Melanie's eye and she wiped it away with the back of her hand.

"I didn't know my father had died. I didn't want to be sent back to him. He told me I had disgraced the family. He said I belonged in some sort of group home for unwed mothers."

Jasper shook his head and my eyes grew misty too.

"Have you seen Trace?" I asked.

"No. Isn't he here in Levi? You said he was here looking for me. I didn't know. I just didn't want to face him or…or anybody."

Patting her hand, I said, "I'm sure he is here somewhere. We haven't seen him for a few days. He will be relieved to know you are safe."

Melanie pushed back her chair.

"Thank you for the coffee, the food, and the use of your basement. I'll go now."

"And where will you go, young lady?" Mom asked.

"I…I don't know. Somewhere."

Miss Georgia got up, went to Melanie, and placed her hands on the young girl's shoulders.

"You most certainly are not going anywhere. If you are not going to think about yourself, think about your baby. This old house is too big for my sister and me. We've got rooms upstairs just waiting to be lived in again. You are going to stay right here with us and let us take care of you."

Mom, Jasper and I stared at Miss Georgia. Miss Carolina smiled and nodded. Melanie looked up at Miss Georgia with something close to reverence. Slowly, she took the old, wrinkled hand that rested on her shoulder.

"Thank you," she whispered. "You are very good."

Jasper grinned from ear to ear. "Didn't I tell you?" he said. "Didn't I tell you these ladies are the best in the world?"

Drawing a deep breath, I shook my head. Never would I have imagined one of our mysteries would be solved in this way. Nobody but God could have planned such an ending.

Chapter 33

"Me? Level-headed?" Amy laughed. "This is the first time I've been accused of *that*."

I laughed too, but it was true. Amy Smith Miller might come up with some zany ideas, like the ghost walk the night of our housewarming, but in between those times, she was a pretty straight thinker.

"You can see things as they are," I said, picking up little Darcy Ann and settling her onto my lap. The twins—my namesake and her brother Drew—had grown inches since I last saw them. I made a silent vow to visit more often as Amy's children grew up.

"It's about Grant, isn't it?" Amy asked, taking a plastic ball out of her son's mouth.

"Why do you think that?" I asked. "Can't best friends get together for a chat without one of them becoming suspicious?"

Shaking her head, Amy said, "Just about the only time you make the drive out here to the ranch, is because you want to discuss that handsome lawman of yours."

"Mine? I would say he's not. But that brings up the subject. I'm afraid Grant is going to ask me to marry him."

"Why, that's wonderful!" Amy said. "You two should have been married a long time ago. I told you that! You have so much in common and, I think, despite your first marriage and all those years in between, you still love each other."

I set Darcy Ann on the floor beside her brother.

"That's the problem. Jake always stands between us even though he's gone. I can't forget him, Amy."

"Who said you should?" she asked. "Of course you will never forget him. He was a big part of your life for years."

I grabbed a sofa cushion and started braiding the fringe. "You don't understand. I think I still love him."

She stared at me for a full twenty seconds without saying a word. This must have been a record for Amy.

"Want a Coke?" she asked.

Amy was the only person of my acquaintance who offered Cokes instead of tea or coffee.

"Oh, for Pete's sake, Amy! Don't change the subject."

She clinked ice into glasses. "I'm not changing the subject. I'm thinking."

"Okay, well, don't take all day."

Handing me a frosty glass, she sat beside me.

"Do you mind if I say something?"

The soft drink tasted cool, sweet, and refreshing. "My goodness, no! That's why I came."

Amy shook her head at Drew. "You have your orange juice, honey. Cokes are not good for little fellows." Turning to me, she said, "I think the arrival in town of your handsome preacher has brought back memories of Jake, and you are feeling torn."

So Amy had noticed the resemblance too. My sip of Coke caught in my throat. I coughed and sputtered. "Well, I never heard of..."

Amy grinned. "I'm right, am I not?"

"Okay. You're maybe about halfway right, but isn't that dumb? I feel so stupid."

Amy quirked an eyebrow. "You shouldn't, you know. Love can play tricks on a person."

"How would you know?" I asked. "You and Jack have been happily married for years. You have a wonderful marriage."

Amy stared down at her glass. "Yes, we do. Now. But, have you forgotten my marriage to Rex?"

"As a matter of fact, I had for a moment. Sorry."

Amy's first marriage occurred while Jake and I were living in Dallas. Now I remembered her phone calls and her tears.

One corner of her mouth quirked up. "It's okay. Sometimes I forget too. Yes, Jack and I have a great marriage, Darcy. It's too bad, though, that past memories can't be simply erased. The only thing I can tell you is that Trace Hughes, as handsome and appealing as he is, is not Jake. Neither is he Grant. With a little encouragement from you, I think Trace would gladly be at your beck and call. My advice is to go slowly. Grant has loved you forever. Love is enduring but it is also fragile. You shouldn't take that lightly."

"It's not just my fickle heart, Amy. Grant is married to his job. He is a lawman. When trouble happens anywhere in the county, he drops whatever, and off he goes! I would always take second place. Besides, his job is dangerous. What if he is killed? I don't think I could stand being a widow a second time."

Amy sighed. "Life has no guarantees. We need to cherish those we love for what time we are allotted. The past is over and done with, Darcy. You can't bring it back through Trace Hughes. No one is assured of the future. What we have is the present. You know that, as well as I do."

"Yes," I said, squeezing her hand. "I do know. Thanks for reminding me."

We clinked glasses.

"Hey!" she said. "That's what friends are for."

"Do you remember the time we double-dated at the old drive-in north of town? I was with Grant and you were with…I forgot his name."

Grinning, she said, "Brad Dennis. Yes, I remember. We saw a re-run of a re-run. It was *Gone With the Wind* and we both started crying at the end when Rhett walked away. Brad got mad and said he didn't see anything to cry about and Rhett Butler was nothing special."

Laughing so hard I wiped tears from my eyes, I said, "Those were fighting words! And when Brad called us dumb broads, Grant told him he'd better watch his mouth and Brad shoved him and Grant yanked him out of the car."

Amy nodded. "Some of the kids spilled out of their cars and started yelling, 'Fight, fight' and the manager came and told us we'd better leave."

"That was some double date! Did you ever go out with Brad again?"

"Are you kidding? No, never! What a dweeb. I'm glad you thought of that, Darcy. Grant was your champion then, and to my way of thinking, he still is."

Slipping to the floor, I gathered the twins in my arms, and gave them a quick squeeze.

"You're right, as usual," I said. "Level-headed with sound advice, that's you, Amy."

"Any advice I have, Darcy, is given with the best intentions 'cause I love you too, dear friend."

Chapter 34

Tossing and turning that night, I watched the hands of my bedside clock creep to midnight, then one. Finally, I could lie there no longer. Easing from under the sheet so I would not disturb Jethro, I slid from bed and padded to the window. Moonlight lit the herb garden and dark woods beyond. Through the open window came the roar of swollen Lee Creek. I hoped our new bridge was sturdy enough to withstand the force of the water. July's unprecedented rains would certainly test the strength of the sturdy timbers.

My mind would not shut off the images of recent happenings. The excitement of finding that the ghost was none other than Melanie Hughes still had my adrenalin pumping. And Jasper—why was that young man always at the heart of so many puzzles? Hopefully, he would go home and Pat would no longer be worried about his whereabouts.

My heart sang with the knowledge that Melanie Hughes was safe with Miss Georgia and Miss Carolina. Now if we could just locate her brother!

Visiting with Amy had an energizing rather than a calming effect. What fun we'd had as teenagers, and how lucky that she and Jack still lived in Ventris County.

Even though my body should have been ready for sleep, my mind would not cooperate. The day had not been conducive for slumber.

Should I go downstairs and brew a cup of tea? Coffee would probably be too much for my agitated nerves.

My mother and I had not made our planned trip to Ben's farm after all. What was happening there? Would the intruder return tonight? If I were he, I would. The ground was soft from the rains, and the moon was bright, a perfect combination for furtive digging.

Was Hiram Schuster on guard at the old cellar, or was he snoozing as Mom was? Perhaps we needed a younger person to act as a guard on the farm. After it became a school, a guard would most certainly be in order. With a sinking feeling, I realized that curiosity about what lay buried on the farm would be an ongoing problem.

At last, I reached a decision. Just as this night would be a good one for digging, it would also be perfect for an investigative reporter to go take a look.

I had to know whether someone was continuing to dig into that buried cellar on the farm. No way would I disturb my mother's sleep and ask her to go with me. I would leave a note by her coffee pot and pray that I got back home before she woke up and found it.

I stepped into jeans, pulled on a red, short-sleeved knit top, and slipped into a black, long-sleeved cotton shirt. Shod in socks and black boots, I was ready to make the trek to Ben's farm.

After scribbling the note to Mom, I picked up my purse, eased open the back door, and tiptoed to the garage. My niggling voice of common sense asked me if I was in my right mind, going off alone in the dead of night with no plan except to see if that mystery trespasser was hard at work. I silenced that pesky voice by telling it that if I found someone digging, I would merely return to my car and call Grant.

Bright moonlight lit my way. I turned off the car's lights until safely across our bridge, and again as the Ventris farm came in sight. Thankfully, my car was not white. I hoped I would not be visible to anyone busy with digging. Nothing but the moon guided me into Ben's driveway.

No light shone in the main house, and only a dim glow lit the bunk house. I felt sure Hiram left that bulb burning night and day.

I slid out of the Escape with my flashlight and cell phone, gently pushed the door shut, and gazed around the yard. If Hiram was awake, he might already be at the cellar site.

Slipping from tree to bush, I walked as softly as my boots allowed. It's funny how weird things look at night, how lonely and hushed, as if the familiar landscape were an alien planet with no life on it except mine.

Stopping in the shadow of the farmhouse, I listened; no sound of pickax or shovel disturbed the night. Even the animal and insect noises of the surrounding woods seemed stilled.

Looking behind me, then right and left, I scurried through the yard until I reached the stone wall dividing the yard from the barnyard. Sinking down behind the wall, I peered over the top at the rounded knoll, beneath which rested secrets Mom and I did not want shared with anybody besides those who already knew, which amounted to Grant Hendley and Jasper Harris. It seemed like eons ago that my mother and I had fled from that cellar with its contents, barely escaping with our lives. I swallowed the bitter, metallic taste which rose in my mouth at those thoughts.

Bending close to the ground, I darted toward the filled-in cellar, flicking on the flashlight and beaming it downward.

My toe caught in a freshly-dug ditch. Stumbling, I staggered to my knees as I heard a slight movement behind me. Pain ricocheted off my head and spread down my neck and shoulders. A thousand lights exploded behind my eyelids. Darkness deeper than any night closed around me.

Chapter 35

I tried to swat away the annoying light that beamed into my eyes, but my hand did not want to cooperate. A hazy cloud of faces gazed down at me: worried faces, stern faces ... and someone pounded a drum directly into my ears.

My lips felt dry and my tongue refused to form words. I wanted to ask, "What happened?" but all I could manage was a hoarse bleat, "Wha-a?"

"She's awake. Thank God," Mom said, her voice choked with tears.

"We'd better call an ambulance," Grant said.

"No, wait." I recognized the voice of Dr. McCauley. "I think she just received a glancing blow to the back of her head. Grant, can you carry her into Hiram's front room and put her on the sofa?"

"Sure, sure. That's the ticket. Get her off the cold, wet ground." This voice surely belonged to Hiram Schuster.

"Can walk," I muttered.

"Hush," said Grant. Slowly and gently, he lifted me until my head rested against his shoulder. I felt his heart beating against my face as he carried me to Ben Ventris's farmhouse.

Placing me on the sofa, Grant adjusted the pillow Hiram handed him, and Mom pulled an afghan up to my chin.

"Really," I muttered. "I'm not dead. I'm all right. Will somebody tell me what happened?"

Dr. McCauley placed a tablet against my lips and held a glass of water toward me.

"Take this," he said. "It will help your headache."

Hopeful that the drumbeat in my ears would subside, I did as the doctor ordered.

"Grant?" I questioned.

He knelt on the floor beside the sofa and took my hand.

"When your mother found your note, she phoned me. I brought her out here. Jim drove behind us. We got here as soon as we could, but evidently not before somebody gave you a hard knock on the head. Your mom phoned the doctor. Why'd you do it, Darcy? Why did you come out here alone? Of all the foolhardy..."

Jim? Jim Clendon was actually here? Turning my head a fraction, I saw Grant's deputy standing near the door of the living room, twisting his hat round and round. Jim was never my favorite person, but it touched me that he had come to my rescue. In fact, it was such a poignant moment that I began to cry.

"Now, Grant! Look what you've done!" Mom said. "Don't cry, Darcy. It's going to be all right."

Hiccupping slightly, I closed my eyes. Doc McCauley had the most wonderful medicine. Feeling warm and protected, I dozed off, thankful that the Lord watched over me and grateful for each of the people around me.

It was daylight when I opened my eyes. Mom lay stretched out in Hiram's recliner. Grant lay on the floor beside my sofa, his head on a cushion and an afghan covering him. Dr. McCauley dozed in the second recliner. Looking at these, my family and friends, I felt a stab of conscience for putting myself into danger and causing them worry.

Hiram evidently had gone to bed and Jim had gone, probably to the office in town.

Raising my head from the pillow, I felt a stab of pain along the back of my neck and my shoulder. I groaned and immediately the three other people in the room opened their eyes and stared at me.

Doctor McCauley banged down the recliner's footrest and limped to the sofa.

"Slept with my leg in a twist," he said. "How're you feeling?" He took his stethoscope from around his neck.

"Better," I muttered.

"Hmm. Heart is all right. No fever. Follow my finger with your eyes."

I did that to the doctor's satisfaction, after which he beamed a narrow light into my eyes.

"Let's get you up and see how your head feels," he said.

After I sat, stood, and took a couple of steps with no problems, the doctor told me I'd live.

"Just take it easy for a few days," he said. "And come to my office, soon as you're up to it."

Dr. McCauley left just as Hiram brought coffee.

"You're an angel," I said, taking the steaming cup. Even Mom's coffee never tasted better than Hiram's at that moment.

Mom, Grant, Hiram and I enjoyed the hot caffeine in silence for a few minutes. At last, Grant spoke.

"Darcy, do you remember anything about what happened? Did you hear or see anybody? Smell anything? Just anything at all before you were knocked unconscious?"

I have heard people say it made their heads hurt to think. Well, my head really did start to throb as I thought.

"No one was stirring. I thought Hiram was probably asleep, and..."

"I was asleep," Hiram admitted. "I had worked hard on the bunkhouse, meant to go keep watch but I sat down on that sofa there and just conked out. Sorry, Darcy."

"Anyway, the only thing I heard was, actually, nothing. No crickets, no owls, no rustling in the bushes. Everything was really quiet. I didn't see anybody, so I walked toward the cellar, stumbled over a ditch, and fell. That's all I remember. Except the headache. Oh, that blow hurt."

"Probably stumbling saved your life. I'll go back after good daylight and take a look around," Grant said. "Miss Flora, can you drive Darcy home?"

Mom nodded. "Of course."

"I'll help you to your car, Darcy. Promise that you'll go straight to bed when you get home. D'you hear?"

"Yes, sir," I said. Bossy Grant. Always giving orders, but this time they sounded rather endearing. And I planned to obey.

Chapter 36

I spent the rest of the day in my bedroom. It was wonderful to snuggle under the sheets, Jethro beside me, and doze. Why does trauma make a person tired? I was as limp as a dishrag.

The next day, however, visitors started arriving. I had not expected this; neither had my mother. I thought we were going to keep quiet about someone digging at Ben's farm. We sure didn't want to contribute to the rumor of buried treasure. Somehow, however, word leaked out that Darcy Campbell was injured. Levi was better than the internet for spreading gossip or half-truths.

I was drinking coffee in the kitchen when Pat came, bringing a bowl of tomato soup.

"So, Darcy, what happened to you? The way I heard it, you stumbled and hit your head on a stick of firewood when you went out to the school that Flora's building on Ben's farm. How on earth could you have stumbled on a stick of wood? Doesn't Hiram keep things a little neater than that? My goodness! I would have thought he'd have the wood in a nice wood box…" Pat ran out of breath and looked questioningly at Mom.

I did not know who first told the story of my night attacker, maybe Hiram or Jim? If anybody mentioned it while sitting in Dilly's café, it would spread like wildfire over town. Looking at Mom, I tried to think of a possible explanation. Surprisingly, she laughed.

"Oh, my goodness! Pat, rumors sure have a life of their own. Yes, Darcy got a nasty bump on the head, but Dr. McCauley said she's going to be fine. As for stumbling over a stick of firewood, well…"

Deciding this was an opportune moment to jump into the conversation, I started to cough. And cough. Mom ran for a glass of water. Pat pounded me on the back.

Gasping, I changed the subject. "I've been meaning to ask about Jasper. Is he home?"

Pat nodded, her curls bouncing. "More or less. He comes home at night, but right now he is with that little Melanie girl. My Jasper has found another wounded creature to take care of."

"Did he talk to Grant?" Mom asked.

"He did," Pat said. "Grant told him not to hide out anymore or he'd have Murphy trail him up. Jasper believed him, I'm glad to say."

Miss Georgia came and Miss Carolina, bringing a pie. They didn't ask any questions, but their concern for me was evident in their faces.

Jackson Conner stopped in. I suspected he wanted to see that Mom was all right. She gave him a minute-by-minute account of what really happened at the farm. Jackson had heard many Ventris County secrets through the years. We knew that he would keep this one locked away with the others.

Even Burke Hopkins came, bringing us a dozen eggs, just in case we needed more. If he was curious, he did not say anything. He solemnly advised me to be careful; trouble lay all around us. I agreed with that. Trouble and murder and a missing preacher.

My friend Amy phoned, saying her twins had a cold or she would have been to see me, and she was very sorry that I had stumbled off our bridge and hit my head on a rock in Lee Creek.

"It's a wonder you didn't drown, Darcy," she said.

I looked at Mom. "I've never seen anything like this," I said. "These stories are getting more and more interesting."

After he left the office that night, Grant stopped in.

We three—Mom, Grant and I—sat at the dining table enjoying a cup of hot coffee and the pie that the Jenkins twins brought.

Tree shadows lengthened in our yard, and a whippoorwill called from the forest. A family of sparrows which had claimed our honeysuckle vine for a fragrant home, twittered and chirped as they gathered in for the night.

Peace settled like shadows over the forest as the day gave way to evening. Attackers, missing people and murderers seemed alien subjects in the warmth of the kitchen, but they were uppermost on our minds.

"Well, it's just got me stumped," Mom said. "Who would want to hurt Darcy? And why?"

Grant ran his hand over his jaw and shook his head.

"Miss Flora, I'd say the 'why' is because somebody was warning Darcy to stop nosing around. Word has gotten out that she's trying to find Walter's killer. A lot of people know about your trip to Georgia, Darcy. Whoever is digging out there evidently didn't appreciate your company. Or, maybe the guy meant to kill you but you tripped in that ditch as he struck. If she had died, that would have been warning enough for you to back off, Miss Flora."

Mom shuddered and shook her head. "Thank the Lord he didn't succeed," she whispered.

"But who, Grant?" I asked. "Do you think the same person who killed Walter Harris is the one digging at the cellar and the same person who attacked me?"

"If I knew that for sure, I might be able to put another piece in the puzzle," Grant said.

He reached into his jeans pocket.

"I think we can safely say somebody has heard the rumor of what might be buried on Ben's farm," he said. "I was afraid this would happen. A lot of the gossip about Ben Ventris and the legend of Cherokee gold, I lay onto poor old Mort. Mort just couldn't keep his mouth shut. He printed too much in that paper of his and he wasn't too picky about what was fact and what was just talk. I'm afraid somebody heard enough to think there might be something on Ben's farm that's worth finding."

"And now Mort's dead," I said.

Grant nodded. "I went back and looked around that cellar. The ground was all scuffed up by the ditch, but I found this."

He opened his hand. On his palm lay a plastic guitar pick.

I shrugged. "What do you mean you found it? I gave it to you after I found it at the Jenkins house. Do you carry it around with you?"

Mom got up to pour more coffee. "Did you get fingerprints off it?"

Grant frowned and shook his head. "This isn't the pick you found at the Jenkins house, Darcy. This one was on the ground beside the ditch on Ben's cellar where you were attacked. You gave me the first pick. This is the second guitar pick."

I stared at that little triangular piece of plastic, thoughts swirling through my head like moths circling a lamppost.

"This makes no sense, Grant," I said at last. "Of course we associate that pick with Trace Hughes, but Trace wouldn't go around dropping guitar picks so he would be a suspect. That's crazy."

Grant's eyes narrowed. "Maybe he is crazy. Maybe his sister's disappearance and his father's death did something to his mind."

I gingerly poked the pick with my index finger and Grant dropped it back into his pocket.

"Wait a minute. I don't think Trace is crazy. I don't know why we can't find him, but I believe he has a good reason for not being here. Maybe he's hurt somewhere. And, by the way, Trace can't be the only person in Levi who plays a guitar."

Grant raised his eyebrows and drew a deep breath.

"Maybe. I'm afraid I don't have your confidence in the guy. To start off with, he came to town claiming to be somebody he's not. He was supposed to preach at Walter's funeral and he didn't—didn't even send word. He threatened Mort and Mort wound up dead. I'd say he didn't want Mort to go to Georgia, wouldn't you? Now, we have not one, but two guitar picks. I'm sure there're lots of people in Levi who play a guitar, but they probably hang onto their picks. The thing of it is, Darcy, all these things started happening after Trace Hughes came to town."

I set my empty coffee cup down on the table. I could not believe that Trace Hughes was my attacker at the farm. "So, because you found the pick at Ben's farm and I found the first one at the Jenkiness home, you are thinking Mort's death maybe wasn't an accident?"

Grant nodded as he pushed back his chair.

"That's exactly what I'm thinking," he said.

"Well," I called after him, "at least there wasn't a guitar pick at Old String's shack."

"Not one that we found anyway," Grant flung over his shoulder.

Chapter 37

Trudging into the kitchen, hoping that a cup of coffee was all I needed to feel normal again, I noticed the unusual darkness of the morning. Even the overhead light seemed dim. I felt more like myself today except for still having a lump on my head the size of a goose egg, and feeling so cold my arms prickled. There was something else; an odd feeling kept niggling at me. It was the same way I had felt before last year's earthquake.

Pacing the floor, I glanced at the dripping eaves. Going for a walk sometimes relaxed me, but it was not a day to be outside. Why did my nerves feel like a tightly-strung wire? Had I consumed too much caffeine, or was the continual rain getting to me? Maybe it was a delayed reaction to the attack. A low roar came and went in my ears, probably an aftermath of the blow to my head.

I had not put my car into the garage the previous night. It sat in the driveway, a dark oblong shape through the gray rain. Today, I planned to go to Levi and visit with Melanie Hughes. Maybe she could tell me something—anything—that would suggest the whereabouts of her brother. She might actually know something, some clue, without realizing she knew it. This is what I hoped to glean from Melanie.

Glancing out the back door, I saw my mother, raincoat thrown over her head, coming out of the chicken house. She splashed through puddles in the yard, jumped up on the porch and, leaving her coat on the back of a lawn chair, hurried into the house, shaking water from her hair. Stepping out of her soaked shoes, she padded barefoot down the hall to the bathroom.

"Those eggs are finally hatching under the setting hen," she called. "I heard some faint peeping from the baby chicks, but was afraid to reach under her, afraid I might hurt one of the babies. Besides, her yellow eyes didn't look friendly."

"How do you think Jethro is going to react to those little chickens?" I asked. "He may not know that they are not to play with, or worse yet, they might look to him like small, feathered snacks on two legs."

Hearing his name, Jethro opened one eye, flexed his paws and returned to napping on the cushioned seat of the rocking chair.

Coming back to the kitchen wearing her house shoes, Mom went to the coffee pot and poured a fresh cup of brew.

"I imagine those babies' mother will discourage Jethro if he gets too close," she said. "Like most mamas, that old hen will be pretty protective of her chicks."

I refreshed my own coffee and sat down opposite her at the table.

She held her cup with both hands and shivered.

"I'm going to take a good look at that old sewing machine today," she said. "It needs to be dusted and I want to pull out all the drawers and give it a going over. Who knows? Maybe Jeff Thorne left a letter in there. Or, there might be a card of antique pins. Anyway, I've been wanting to really examine it, and this seems like a good day."

Leaving my coffee, I walked to the sewing machine and pushed it close to the table.

"Jeff kept the wheels oiled," I said. "It rolls easily."

Mom sipped her coffee. "Lee Creek has a strange sound to it this morning. It must have risen a foot during the night. I'm glad we have a bunch of groceries, because the water is almost up to our bridge. We may be marooned here for a while if the rain keeps up."

I put down my cup. "You're kidding."

Trotting to the front porch, I could hardly believe the scene in front of me. Lee Creek, our pleasant, clear little stream, was quiet no longer.

Its muddy waters foamed and tossed. Over-running its banks, it surged against the lower part of the yard, lapping hungrily at the grass. Only a few more inches would put it over the bridge. No longer a pleasant accompaniment to the sounds of nature, it thundered like a hundred runaway horses.

"Darcy, look!" Mom said, grasping my arm. "There's a car coming this way."

"Not in this weather!" I said. "Who in the world would be out today?"

As the vehicle neared, I recognized the truck that our lawn person, Tim Johnson, drove. He pulled into our drive, got out and galloped toward the house, a long, dark object in his hands.

"Mr. Johnson!" I said. "Our grass is more a river than a lawn! Surely you aren't going to mow."

Jumping up onto the porch, he grinned at us.

"I know. I'm just plain crazy, I guess, but all this rain gives me the heebie jeebies. I left my mower in your garage last time I was here. Had to take off the blade to sharpen it. I haven't been able to mow any grass for a long time, so I've been working on my equipment. I sharpened this blade and if it's all right with you, I'll just go out to the garage and put it on today. It'll give me something to do."

He held the blade gingerly by one end, his hands protected by heavy work gloves.

"Sure, it's all right," Mom said, "but I wouldn't advise you to stay long because Lee Creek is on the rise."

"This little job won't take long," Mr. Johnson assured us.

"Come on in for a cup of coffee," Mom said. "I think there's enough in the pot for you to take a big mugful to the garage with you."

He held the door for us and we trooped inside.

"Mighty nice house you got here," he said, following Mom and me to the kitchen.

"Thanks," I answered.

Jethro took one look at the newcomer, jumped from his chair and disappeared somewhere in the house.

Rummaging through the cabinet, I found a tall travel mug.

"This should work," I said, going to the coffee pot.

"I don't want your coffee," Mr. Johnson said.

My ears must have been affected by the noise of the flooding creek. I turned from the cabinet to face him.

"What did you say?"

"I said that I don't want your coffee nor nothin' in this kitchen except information. You all and your high-falutin' ways. What I want is to know a few things and I'm going to get answers, one way or the other."

I did not recognize our cheerful, Santa Claus-look-alike lawn person in the glowering man who stood before us. His white eyebrows drew down and his eyes glinted with malice. My breath caught in my throat. Instinctively, I grabbed my mother's hand.

Holding the lawn mower blade in both hands like a battering ram, Johnson took a step toward us.

Chapter 38

Backing away from this menace, I tried to think sanely. Surely this was a nightmare and was not actually happening. However, the red, glowering face with hate-filled eyes seemed real enough that I wanted as far away from him as possible.

We bumped into the sewing machine. Johnson stopped and eyed us. Was he trying to figure out his next move? I couldn't seem to gulp enough air, and my arms and legs felt frozen. What did safety manuals say about attackers with lawn mower blades? I wished for Dad's pistol, but it was far away in a drawer in the next room. Should I try to keep him talking? It was worth a try.

Licking my lips, I said, "Umm, Mr. Johnson, why are you angry? What have we done to you?"

He laughed, a low, caustic rumble.

"What did you do? Why, maybe you, yourself, didn't do anything. That's the way it is with you people, isn't it? You're not to blame for anything. You've got everything…nice house, in fact, two houses! Now ain't that grand? The way I hear it, you've got gold and jewels and who knows what hidden away somewhere, maybe out there at that school of yours, and you're going to tell me where it is. Me? I ain't never had anything except an old man who beat me, a ma who took off and left me, and a whole lot of hard knocks."

To my horror, Mom shook her finger at him.

"You're just a mean old man, Tim Johnson! None of those things made you turn out bad. Think about what you're doing. Gold and jewels? Do you see any gold and jewels around here? Do you want to spend a whole lot of time in jail for killing two defenseless women?"

"Mom," I gasped. Killing two women? She was talking about us, and I didn't think mentioning this man's intentions was a really good idea at the moment.

Johnson grinned, but his eyes narrowed to slits.

"I've already spent time in the slammer. That's where I met your old pal Walter Harris. Walter got to talking about the buried gold stories. Said he knew all about it, bein' from here. I decided to throw in with him and we'd come and see if we could find it. Only thing is, Walter got cold feet. He decided maybe he'd like to stick around close to his wife and that goofy son of his. When a man starts to back out on a deal, next thing he'll be squealin' to the sheriff about us poking around for gold. I'd been having my doubts about Walter anyhow. He didn't seem to know much about the gold's location, no more than I did. And, if I found it, why should I have to share it with Walter?"

The question escaped my stiff lips before I could stop it.

"Did you kill Walter?"

"Oh, yep. Yep, sure did. Funny thing. I found a knife right there in that old shack. Picked it up and stabbed him before Walt knew what was happenin'." A thoughtful look crossed his face. "Maybe I was a bit hasty, but the opportunity presented itself—so to speak—and, truth is, I'd killed old Walter before I thought."

It's odd how I reacted to this shock. Since nothing taking place in that kitchen could possibly be real, I asked another question.

"And Mort? You surely didn't kill him! That porch railing came loose and he fell."

A sly, knowing grin slid across Johnson's face.

"Well, now, it's a funny thing about those old porch railings. They do come loose sometimes, 'specially with a little help. Mort was a worse gossip than an old woman, but some people are always ready to listen—

the sheriff, for instance. If Mort had told the Jenkins women what he dug up about me, about my jail record, and a few other things I've been accused of, do you think those women woulda kept their mouths shut? Maybe he did tell 'em. They were going to be next on my list, just to make sure. Then, I figured you probably know more about that gold than anybody else, since it's supposed to be on your land."

He paused and pointed to his head.

"Me? I'm always on my toes. I had a perfect right to be at those old maids' house, didn't I? I took care of their lawn. Well, maybe I just took care of Mort too. Worked out pretty good. What did you think about me droppin' that guitar pick? Pretty smart, huh?"

"You?" The word came out on a hiss of air. "You dropped that pick? Why? Where did you get it?"

Johnson laughed and a chill ran down my spine.

"That's for me to know. You'll never find your preacher-man. I knew he'd come in handy some way. Too trusting. Left the door of his house wide open and I walked right in and helped myself to a handful of guitar picks. Bein' a preacher, he's supposed to bring light into darkness, ain't he? Well, he'll have a mighty hard time bringing light into the darkness where he's at, that is, if he could move around at all, which he can't."

"But enough talk," he growled, baring his teeth like a hungry wolf. "I want to know the location of that gold. Are you going to tell me or do you need a little persuasion?"

"You can't kill us," I said. "Who would tell you about the gold then?"

He leered at us. "Maybe if I killed just one of you, the other would talk. I kind of like that idea."

Mom's hand in mine shook and felt icy cold. "Actually, we can't tell you where the gold is," she said. "We'll have to show you. Both of us. Together. If you kill one of us, believe me, you'll regret it to your dying day, which might be sooner than you think if you harm my daughter."

Glancing at my mother's face, I saw determination in the hard line of her mouth. She meant every word.

"Oh, I'm so scared!" he jeered. "No, you're gonna tell me now! I'm not foolin'. I don't have time for games. You might save your lives if you tell me where it is. I'm gonna find it, one way or the other!"

As Tim Johnson spoke, Mom and I inched around Jeff Thorne's sewing machine. Now we had the old machine between us and what looked like certain death. With a low snarl, Johnson raised the mower blade with both hands and lunged toward us.

Instinct took over. Releasing my mother's hand, I shoved the sewing machine at him the instant he swung the blade.

The old machine rammed into Johnson. Surprise widened his eyes. With a grunt and what I suspected was a vicious oath, he fell backward. The downward arc of the heavy blade whipped past my face. Deflected by the ancient cabinet, it splintered the wood, bounced off and whacked Johnson's thigh. He yelled, grabbed his leg and dropped like a rock.

"Come on, Mom!" I shouted. "Run!"

Hand in hand, we skirted the fallen man and darted out the back door. Rain and wind struck us like a wall. Mom slipped and fell.

"I lost my house shoe!" she wailed as I pulled her out of a puddle.

Glancing over my shoulder, I saw Tim Johnson struggling to regain his feet. My heart in my mouth, I splashed through the rain, pulling my mother along. Jerking open the doors of my SUV, we scrambled inside. Johnson would be after us if he did not bleed to death first.

Chapter 39

"Faster, Darcy, faster!" Mom yelled as I rammed the car into reverse, backed out of the driveway and, tires spinning on the wet gravel, aimed for our bridge.

In the few minutes since Tim Johnson's arrival, the creek had risen. It now poured across the bridge. Saying a prayer that the raging water would not wash us downstream, I pressed on the accelerator and drove onto the planks. Thankful that I knew it so well, I could only guess where the bridge ended and the stream began. Catching us like a giant hand, the heavy current pushed us sideways. The tires lost traction.

"Dear Lord," I prayed aloud, "don't let the engine drown."

Trying to drive across Lee Creek was a living nightmare in which we ran from a pursuer in slow motion. I stomped the accelerator. The struggling engine revved, but our speed stayed the same. We were being swept ever closer to the edge of the bridge and the thundering current of the creek.

It seemed an eternity before we reached the road.

"Oh, thank God. Thank God," Mom breathed.

Glancing at my rearview mirror, I expected to see Johnson's truck behind us. However, all I saw were sheets of gray rain.

Mom's head swiveled from front to back. We both expected at any second to see headlights gaining on us.

The flight through the storm toward Levi would forever be etched in my memory. Wind-lashed trees bent toward the road and reached out for the car. Windshield wipers did almost no good; the deluge pounded us. We skidded sideways and slid helplessly toward the overflowing ditches. But, somehow, the Escape righted itself and we kept going at breakneck speed through the dark woods of Ventris County toward the safety of Levi and Grant Hendley.

At last the road became the main street of town. Dear, safe, familiar landmarks appeared through the rain. Lights inside the sheriff's office glowed a welcome. I swung into a parking spot, braked, and leaned my head against the steering wheel.

"Whew!" I whispered. "I don't know if I have the strength to open the door."

"Well, I do," Mom declared. "Come on, Darcy. We aren't safe until we get inside those four walls."

The sight of two wet, muddy, gasping, frightened females, one of them wearing only one house shoe, brought Grant's secretary Doris Elroy to her feet, her eyes wide and her mouth dropping open. Bursting through Grant's door, I ran to him and his arms went around me, pulling me close, wet shirt and all.

Mom and I gulped out the horrendous experience and our close brush with death. We told Grant about the transformation of Tim Johnson, his threat with the lawn mower blade, our flight across the bridge, and the terrifying drive into Levi.

Grant's face grew white then red as Mom and I told our unbelievable story.

Doris collected two blankets from somewhere and two cups of blessedly hot coffee. Draping the blankets over our shoulders, she retreated to the door but hovered in the room like an anxious parent. Grant, his arms around both Mom and me, led us to the chairs facing his desk.

"Are you all right?" he asked, kneeling in front of us. "Miss Flora? Did he harm you at all?"

Mom's laugh was shaky. "It's a wonder our heads are still attached, but no, Grant, he didn't hurt us. The only casualties were my old sewing machine and Mr. Johnson's leg. We didn't wait to see how badly either of them was hurt."

"Take care of them, Doris," Grant said, turning to his secretary. He grabbed his hat from a peg on the wall, shrugged into his jacket, and headed for the door.

"Jim!" he bellowed, stepping into the outer office.

I tried to stop him. "Grant, don't go out in this storm. The creek—you can't get over the bridge. You'll drown."

"I'll be fine, Darcy," he said, striding toward the door.

Jim appeared, and the two lawmen dashed out into the rain-filled morning.

Chapter 40

The fireplace in our Levi house radiated a most welcome warmth. My chilled feeling may have been due partly to rain-cooled air and damp clothing, but mostly to shock. The fireplace had been damaged in last year's earthquake but, after being repaired, it burned as cheerfully as ever. We had found several sticks of dry wood in a basket by the front door and coaxed them into a blaze to take the dampness out of the living room. With the doors securely locked, we began to relax.

"It's like old times, isn't it?" Mom asked, holding out her hands to the flames. "This seemed the best place to come, since we can't go back home and Pastor Hughes isn't here. I don't think he would mind."

Standing up, I turned my back to the burning logs, relishing the welcome heat.

"No, of course he wouldn't mind. It is, after all, still our house and we don't know where Trace is."

Mom had found a pair of Trace's socks, and these replaced her one ruined house shoe. Now, she got up to rummage around the kitchen.

"I feel strange poking through his things," she said, "sort of like an intruder, but I'd sure like to perk a pot of coffee."

"I hope you do," I said. "The coffee Doris gave us was hot, but not nearly as strong as the coffee you make."

Soon the aroma of fresh-perked coffee joined the fragrance of wood smoke. We settled in front of the fireplace, holding our cups of hot caffeine.

Rain continued to fall, but not nearly as hard as earlier. A strip of blue sky appeared under the clouds to the west.

Mom yawned. "I could almost close my eyes and doze off. Now, isn't that strange? We just escaped death by inches and were nearly swept away in a flood; there's a madman somewhere out there who's killed two people and wants to kill us, and here I am, getting sleepy."

"It's a reaction to what we've been through," I said. "Our nerves were on overload and now we are safe, at least for the moment. I wish Grant and Jim had waited about going out in the storm. I keep wondering where they are and if they've found Johnson. I don't know what Grant hoped to do. He sure couldn't cross Lee Creek. You know, I've been thinking about what Tim Johnson said."

Mom swallowed her coffee. "How could we forget any of it? I'd like to, but I don't think I ever will. He said a lot. What were you thinking about in particular?"

Trying to sort my thoughts as I talked, I recalled Johnson's exact words.

"We know part of this puzzle," I said. "He confessed to killing Walter and more or less admitted he killed Mort. Remember what he said about Trace?"

"Yes, yes, I think I do. He said Trace was too trusting. He must have just walked right into this house. He could have gotten any number of Trace's guitar picks to drop around and make it look like Trace is guilty of the murders and the attack on you, Darcy. Oh, Dear Lord, he must have been the one who knocked you out."

Emotion choked Mom's voice, and I gripped my cup harder. She was right. That detestable man surely was the one digging on the old cellar and the one who knocked me senseless. How close to death I must have been!

"Yes, I'm sure he was my attacker. Either Johnson was just bragging or he knows where Trace is. Maybe if Grant finds Johnson, he'll make him tell what he did with our preacher."

At long last, my hands stopped shaking. With the paralysis of fear leaving my brain, I was able to think more clearly. Trace had not been seen since before Walter Harris's funeral. Johnson had purposely dropped the guitar picks to make Trace appear guilty of murder and of the attack on me.

"Mom," I said, setting my empty coffee cup on the hearth, "I think Johnson is holding Trace prisoner and I have a pretty good idea where!"

Mom sloshed coffee as she put her cup beside mine.

"You do? Where?"

"Okay, let's try thinking like Johnson. We know he killed Walter Harris out at Old String's shack. He used the knife that Jasper dropped. He said something about Trace not being able to bring light into darkness."

Pausing, I thought back to the day when Old String's shack burned. Part of it was left standing, a couple of walls and a section of roof which collapsed down over them to form a small room. Such a space would certainly be a prison for a victim who was tied up.

Grabbing Mom's arm, I said, "Old String's shack. Part of it wasn't burned. You know how criminals are said to return to the scene of the crime? What if Johnson slipped in here, into this very house, held a gun on Trace or knocked him out or something and took him to that lean-to, the place where he killed Walter. Maybe Trace is there right now!"

Mom stared at me, shaking her head. "I don't know, Darcy. Why would Johnson do that? What did he have against Trace? Mort and Walter were threats, but Pastor Hughes?"

"Because he needed a scapegoat. He was trying to set him up to look guilty of Walter Harris's murder. Maybe he killed Trace already or maybe he didn't. Maybe he thought Trace would be useful some way. We've got to try and find him."

Mom folded her arms and shook her head.

"No. That's silly. We are going to wait for Grant. What if Tim Johnson went back out to that lean-to? You know he'd relish a second chance to kill us."

Pulling on my wet shoes, I grabbed my purse.

"You're right, Mom. You stay here and tell Grant where I'm going."

She stared at me for a moment, shook her head and started upstairs.

"Where are you going?" I called.

"I'm going to borrow a pair of Trace's boots. In for a penny, in for a pound. I'm wearing his socks and drinking his coffee so I might as well wear his boots. They'll be too big, but I don't fancy walking around outside in these socks. Don't you dare leave without me!"

Chapter 41

Roadside ditches, looking like small creeks, ran brimful of water, but at least we didn't have to cross Lee Creek or the Ventris River to reach the shack. The rain had stopped, and a weak sun peeked apologetically through the clouds.

Turning the Escape onto the faint track that was once Old String's driveway, I drove slowly up to the burned-out remains of his house.

"Darcy, look!" Mom gripped my arm and pointed.

Nothing upright remained of the building. The partial walls and roof lay collapsed on the ground.

My heart turned over, and tears burned my eyes. If Trace had been under the heavy lumber, it would undoubtedly have killed him when it fell.

"Don't say it. There's a chance he's alive," Mom said. I shut off the engine and we jumped out of the car, sloshing through streams of water and stumbling over charred boards.

"Trace! Trace!" I called, clawing at the debris.

My only answer was the dripping trees and our own breathing.

"Help me with this rafter," Mom said.

Together, we grabbed the heavy board and hefted it to the side.

At last, the corner of the house that had belonged to Ventris County's recluse lay bare and dismantled on the ground. And empty. Trace was not there.

Breathing hard, I swiped my damp hair out of my eyes and sank down on the wet grass.

"Thank God he is not here. But where is he, Mom? He's got to be somewhere. Maybe Johnson killed him and buried him. He said that Trace is in a dark place, and nothing gets much darker than a grave."

We slogged back to my car and climbed inside.

"Yes, he must be somewhere, even if he is dead. But you know, Darcy, my spirit is willing but all of a sudden I feel as weak as a kitten. I've had about enough for one day. Let's go back to the house in town and rest."

Glancing at her pale, strained face, my conscience pricked me.

"You're right, Mom. I'm so sorry. Of course you're tired. So am I. I'm pretty sure Lee Creek is still rolling over the bridge and we couldn't go home even if we knew Johnson wasn't there. Let's go back to the town house, see if Trace left bread and peanut butter, and then go to bed."

"We'll feel more like tackling this puzzle tomorrow," Mom agreed.

My mind, however, would not let go of the question of Trace Hughes. Where was he? What, exactly, had Tim Johnson said? Something about Trace having a hard job bringing light into darkness. Why? Could he be in the attic of our house? No, surely he would have made some sort of noise when he heard us downstairs. Besides, that attic had a window; it wasn't all that dark.

"You know, Darcy, I was thinking about all the strange happenings of this week. We may not have found Trace, but I'm sure glad we found his sister! Just think about that child being down in the twins' dark basement. Even with a lantern, I imagine she felt like she was living in a cave," Mom said.

"That's it!" I shouted, whacking the steering wheel with my hand. "You're a genius, Mom."

"Oh, my! What did I say?"

"A cave! A cave is dark, about the darkest thing I know. Do you know of any caves around here?"

Mom rubbed her forehead. "Well, let me see…the only one I know of is that cave on the land Grant just bought from Gil Monroe."

"Right! What if that's what Johnson meant by a 'dark place'?"

Mom's voice trembled. "But, Darcy, that cave is close to the river. We've never had this much rain at one time before. Ever. I'll bet the cave is under water."

Fear gripped me with an icy hand.

"You're right," I whispered. "When Grant and I went out to look at it, the river was way past its banks, and we've had a lot more rain since. When we were there, Grant glimpsed a truck leaving the area. He couldn't tell who it was, and we thought it might have been a sightseer looking at the river. Maybe it was Johnson. Oh, dear Lord! We've got to hurry."

Mom wiped tears from her eyes. "He might have drowned already. Please, Lord, keep Trace Hughes safe."

I stepped on the gas and my little SUV fishtailed on the wet, narrow pavement. Torn between hoping our pastor was in the cave and hoping he wasn't, I headed for the Ventris River, driving like a person possessed.

Chapter 42

"Try calling Grant again," I said to Mom as we barreled along the country lanes, splashing puddles windshield-high.

"All right," agreed Mom. "I've tried several times and, for some reason, the call doesn't go through. I'll try again, but Darcy, can you slow down a little? We can't help anybody if we wind up in the ditch or meet a deer around one of these curves."

We heard the Ventris River before we saw it. A deep, throaty rumble filled the car, an ominous, relentless thunder. The trees thinned as I drove out of the woods and across a cattle guard into Grant's pasture. Before us, spread out over places that had never known a flood, frothed the angry river. Its surging current carried uprooted trees, a tangle of branches and the roof of someone's shed. Most of Grant's newly-acquired ten acres lay under water. The river writhed and tossed like a primeval animal, gnashing at the little knoll where Grant and I had parked and eaten lunch a short time ago. The water ended only a few yards from my car. I had nearly driven into it.

"I don't believe it," Mom breathed, her eyes wide and wondering. "I never thought the Ventris would ever get this big."

"It's over the road," I said. "I can't take the car any closer. We're going to have to go around it as much as we can and walk to the cave."

Grabbing a flashlight from the glove compartment, I slid to the ground and trotted to the front of my SUV. Taking a deep breath, I glanced at my mother, standing beside me.

"You know," I said, "if we have to swim for it, I hope you kick off those boots. If they filled with water, they'd take you straight to the bottom."

She raised her eyebrows and shook her head. Grabbing her hand, I led the way through the soggy grass, the rumble of the river shutting out all other sound.

The closer we got to the cave, the louder grew the flood's clamor. Conversation was useless. I tried not to look at the dirty, yellow-gray water creeping ever nearer.

At last, the mouth of the cave came in sight. Stepping into its darkness, I flicked on the flashlight and beamed it on rock walls and floor.

This underground room muted the noise of the flood. I shivered at the drop in temperature.

"Trace?" I called, my voice echoing eerily. "Are you in here?"

Mom gripped my arm.

"Listen!" she whispered. "I heard something."

Hardly daring to breathe, I stood still, straining my ears. A soft, muffled sound came from the cave's depth.

"Someone is here," I hissed.

"Or some*thing*," Mom said. "Go carefully, Darcy. No telling what's back in there."

Bats! I remembered longago times with Grant in this cave and a quick retreat from those small winged mammals. Shining my light at the ceiling, I shuddered. Bats stuck as thick as burrs on a thistle. They stirred uneasily at the brightness of my flashlight. I fought the urge to run out of this place. If I ever had a phobia, it was bats! They made my skin crawl.

"Maybe they are what we heard," I whispered, hastily beaming the light onto the cave's floor. "We don't want the whole bunch of them to swarm us."

"No, I think it was something else," Mom said. "Come on, Darcy. They won't bother us if we are quiet."

Keeping the light aimed at the floor, I tiptoed deeper into the cavern, holding tightly to Mom's hand. The floor slanted sharply downward before ending at a dripping wall.

Again came the muffled noise. I shone the light in an arc and my breath caught in my throat. Propped against the back wall, his hands and feet tied and mouth gagged, lay Trace Hughes. His motorcycle lay on the floor beside him.

"Pastor Hughes," whispered my mother.

Trace squirmed. He mumbled against his gag, twisting his head from side to side.

"Here, Mom," I said, thrusting the flashlight into her hands. "I'm going to untie him."

Grabbing one end of the gag, I worked at the knot until the dirty piece of cloth finally fell away.

"Darcy," he gasped. "Am I glad to see you and who? Miss Flora? How'd you find me?"

Mom's voice shook. "The good Lord," she whispered.

"Mom, hold that light still. I've got to untie his feet."

Kneeling in front of him, I attacked the rope which held him prisoner. Perspiration dripped from my upper lip. Tim Johnson had taken no chances his prisoner might escape.

Feeling my knees growing wet, I glanced down at the cave floor. The flashlight shone on a steady stream of river water flowing down the incline and pooling around us.

My heart skipped a beat and thudded against my chest.

"Better hurry, Darcy," Mom said. "The flood has reached the cave. We've got to get out of here or we'll drown."

Our voices disturbed the sleeping bats. They stirred, making soft flutterings and weird noises. Were they getting ready to dive bomb us? I plucked feverishly at the knots that held Trace prisoner.

"Save yourselves," he said. "The river is coming in. Go while you've got a chance. I couldn't walk anyway. Too weak."

"No way," I panted. Pulling against the rope's tautness, I felt the knot give. One more tug and Trace's feet were free.

"We'll untie your hands later," I said. "Come on, we'll make it. Try to stand. We'll help you."

With Mom on one side and me on the other, we slid our arms around his waist, and struggled toward the mouth of the cave which was an eerie, gray blob in front of us.

Trace's motorcycle stayed in the cave, a victim of the flood.

We splashed through water rushing down the slanting floor. When at last we staggered into daylight, the swollen river met us. In the short time we had been below ground, it had spread out across the pasture.

I breathed a sigh of relief. At least the water hadn't submerged my car, although it was lapping at the tires.

Trace struggled to put one foot in front of the other. His legs must have been numb from his cramped position but, step by step, he was regaining the use of them.

We waded through knee-deep water. Twigs carried by the current brushed past us. The force of the river tried to pull us along with the rest of the debris. My car grew ever closer. At last, I was able to touch my mud-spattered, beautiful Escape, waiting like an ark to take us to safety.

Opening the back door, Mom and I shoved Trace inside then clambered into the front seat. My arms shook from fatigue. Mom, I was sure, was just as tired. Nobody said a word. I don't think we had the strength for speech as I backed down the road, bumped across the cattle guard and found a wide spot where I turned around. We were heading back to Levi.

Chapter 43

Although Trace objected, I drove him straight to Dr. McCauley's office where the doctor checked him over thoroughly.

"Drink plenty of water," Dr. McCauley prescribed. "Eat a light supper. Take a shower. Go to bed and sleep for the next week."

While Trace was getting his checkup, I called Doris Elroy and told her we had found him. She had had no word from Grant for several hours and, like us, did not know where he and Jim were.

"Don't worry, Darcy," she said. "Grant can take care of himself. So can Jim."

My common-sense self agreed with Doris, but fear is an unreasonable thing. Had Grant drowned? Had Tim Johnson killed him and Jim? What had happened, and why was he not answering his phone calls?

I prayed silently as I drove all three of us to the house in Levi.

Trace laughed at Mom's footwear.

"Those boots look better on you than they do on me, Miss Flora," he said.

"How did you stay alive, Trace?" I asked. "You were in that cave a long time."

"Johnson brought food and water now and then," Trace answered. "You said you found Melanie. I want to hear more. Tell me all about it. When can I see her?"

So we recounted the story of Melanie and Jasper and the Jenkins basement. We told Trace he could see his sister first thing in the morning.

"Thank God she's safe," Trace said. "I can never repay you or those two Jenkins ladies. Or Jasper. Without Jasper, what would she have done? Melanie should never have run away, but Dad could be harsh. He was wrong."

"Why did Johnson kidnap you?" I asked. "Did you know that he was a murderer?"

"During my talk with Mort, he mentioned Johnson. Mort said he not only knew my past, he knew Johnson's too. I didn't know what he meant, but I followed Johnson and saw him doing something to that porch banister at the Jenkinses' house. When he went back to his truck, I asked him what he was doing. Next thing I knew, he had me tied up and I was in his truck. Preachers talk too much."

"But, you're not a real..." I began.

Trace grinned. "Maybe, but I was beginning to get the feel of being a preacher, and I guess I thought I could talk Johnson into confessing."

Mom shook her head and I went to the kitchen. Homey chores didn't require much thought, and I had no answer for Trace's reasoning.

After a supper of canned tomato soup, Trace pulled himself up the stairs for a shower and bed. Mom and I settled down on the two recliners with cups of hot chocolate.

In spite of my worry about Grant, I dozed. A dream of lawn mowers attacking the house with loud, banging motors woke me as I drifted between wakefulness and sleep. My eyes flew open. Everything looked peaceful. Mom snoozed in her chair. The banging came again and I struggled out of the recliner.

"The door," I mumbled. "Somebody is at the door."

Stumbling to the front, I flicked on the outside light. Grant stood on the porch, lifting his hand to knock again.

I pulled open the door and he stepped inside, wrapping his arms around me. All was right with my world. Grant was safe. Tears of relief filled my eyes.

"Darcy, I stopped by the office and Doris told me that you found Trace Hughes. In our cave? Wasn't it under water? What happened?"

I linked my arm in his and we walked to the living room.

"Grant, I tried to call you," Mom said. "What was wrong with your phone?"

"My phone was a victim of the flood," he said. "It's somewhere in the Ventris River. I want to know everything. Got any coffee? I'm about dead on my feet."

"Coffee coming up," Mom said.

Going to the cabinet, I took out three of Trace's mugs and set them on the table. "Grant, I've got to know. Did you find Tim Johnson? Did you lock him up? What happened when you got to our house?"

Grant sat down at the dining table and dropped his hat on the floor. Running his hands through his hair, he drew a deep breath.

"I didn't ever get to your house. Lee Creek was over the bridge. Way over. It'll run down pretty quick, but nobody could have gotten across that bridge. The water won't reach your house, but it's a good thing you built on that little knoll."

"But, what about Johnson? Did you see him?"

"Not until later, Darcy. I don't know how you and Miss Flora got safely across Lee Creek. It must have been the good Lord sent an angel. Anyway, Jim and I had to stop when we got to the bridge. There was no sign of Johnson. Then, we got stuck; took us a while to get back on the road and when we did, Doris was calling with reports of people being stranded and needing help to get out of the way of the flood. Amy's husband almost lost a mare who is about to foal. The poor little mare was stuck in some brush that had been swept down the river. She couldn't get free. Jack had waded out there and was holding her head up out of the water, but he couldn't get her loose. She was scared and Jack needed help bad. Amy was there on the bank, had the twins in the car, but all she could do was call for help. Thank the Lord I hadn't lost my cell phone yet. I tied a rope around my waist and waded out to the mare and Jack while Jim anchored the rope around the truck's bumper. I think it was during that rescue my phone fell into the river."

"And the little mare? And Jack and Amy? Are they all right?" I visualized the scene at the river, muddy water roaring, the mare's scared eyes, and three men determined to save her and her baby.

"Everyone is fine. I wouldn't be surprised, though, if that foal arrives a little early. The mare was pretty stressed."

Grant paused and looked hopefully toward the coffee pot.

"About Johnson—we found his truck where the creek empties into the river. Tim Johnson was still in it. Drowned. He must have tried to follow you over your bridge and didn't make it." Grant shook his head. "You won't have to worry about him anymore."

Mom gasped. "Oh, what a terrible way to die," she whispered.

Turning to the kitchen window, I gazed out at a scene I had known since childhood. Moonlight lit the back yard. Mom's rose bush under the window swayed in a small breeze. Such a peaceful picture, completely removed from the violence of this amazing day. Tim Johnson, dead. Trace Hughes, found. Grant, Mom and I were safe. Truly, an unforgettable day.

The coffee pot signaled it had finished its brewing. I filled our cups and sat down at the kitchen table.

Mom broke the silence. "I guess I feel sort of numb. We didn't even know Tim Johnson was the killer until this morning. And now tonight, he's dead. I'm afraid he wasn't ready to meet God. I wonder, if his life had been different…"

I wondered too, but I confess at the moment I felt more relief than sadness.

"Mom, that man took the lives of two people. When he died, he was trying to add two more victims to his list—us."

Grant shook his head. "She's right, Miss Flora."

"Yes, but still…" Mom began.

Patting her hand, I smiled and said, "Tomorrow, Mom. If you want to get philosophical and try to figure out just where Tim Johnson went wrong, you are going to have to wait until tomorrow. Right now, I don't want to think of anything stronger than this cup of coffee."

"Wait a minute, Darcy," Grant said. "Before you do anything else, I want to know about how you got Hughes out of that cave. You went in, bats and all? I would have thought it was completely under water."

So Mom and I told the story of searching for Trace at Old String's place and then taking a chance that he might be in Grant's cave. As I re-told the rescue, the fatigue I had been fighting all day caught up with me. My eyelids felt as if they had rocks on them. And I didn't protest when Grant said he would go, and that Mom and I should get some sleep.

Chapter 44

The next afternoon, my mother and I decided we would try to go home. Hopefully, Lee Creek had returned to its banks or at least had run down enough so we could cross the bridge.

Trace was with Melanie at the Jenkins home. Grant and Jim were aiding flood victims. Mom and I were pacing the floor.

"Darcy, there's Jethro to think about. Did we leave enough food for him? And that old hen! I'll bet all her eggs have hatched. Did she have enough sense to stay in the chicken house or did she get outside with those babies and let them drown in a puddle? We've just got to go home!"

"You're right. I've been worried about Jethro too. Are you going to wear Trace's boots home?"

"I've pretty well ruined them. Yes, they're all the footwear I have, and I sure don't want to take time to go to a shoe store. I'll buy him another pair to replace these. Let's go."

So we went. I drove a lot more sanely going back to our house than when we had left it. The sun shone, birds sang, and an innocent blue sky arched over the trees. This was a July day at its finest.

As we neared our house, my muscles tensed. Lee Creek still roared and foamed but it no longer covered the bridge. I drove across, trying not to look at the water swirling below me or think of the trauma of yesterday morning. The feeling of terror was too recent, the remembrance of it too fresh.

Driving around the house, I parked in the driveway and glanced at the back porch. The kitchen door stood wide open. Lights shone from door and windows just as they had when we left. What would we find inside?

After being so eager to return home, neither Mom nor I were in a hurry to leave the car.

"Oh, I hope he didn't kill Jethro," Mom whispered, looking toward the back porch.

"That cat is pretty smart," I said. "He hid when Johnson came, and I doubt that he came out of hiding until he knew it was safe."

We slid out of the car and squished through the wet grass. I stepped up on the porch, calling for Jethro.

He did not appear, and he did not answer with his soft meow as he usually did when I called.

The kitchen was empty. An overturned chair, a few spatters of blood, and the splintered sewing machine cabinet were the only signs of our brush with death.

Rolling off a length of paper towel, I dropped it over the blood. I would clean it up later.

Mom sank into a chair, put her hands over her face, and started to cry.

With tears burning my eyes, I patted her shoulder.

"It's all right, Mom. That awful man is gone. We're home. We're safe and I'm going to plug in your coffee pot."

Mom lifted her head. "I feel like we need a prayer or something to make this kitchen clean again. Such evil and violence were here in our pretty new home. How dare that awful man do that to us? It leaves me with a bad feeling."

I measured coffee and water into the pot. Its cheerful perking helped dispel the gloom.

"I agree; we need something to make this room clean again. We're Baptists so we don't have a priest to do a cleansing ceremony and, although Trace would do his best, he isn't a preacher so I guess that leaves us," I said. "Wait! I think I know just the verse."

Trotting to the living room, I picked up a Bible from the book shelf and returned to the kitchen. Sitting down at the table, I opened to the twenty-third chapter of Deuteronomy and read, "'For the Lord thy God walketh in the midst of thy camp.' This is our camp, Mom. It's where we live and God is with us."

"You're right, Darcy. The Lord is in this house, in this kitchen. I'm proud of you for finding that verse."

"And I'm surprised," I said. "Wonder how I knew that? Usually, you are the Scripture expert."

The coffee pot gurgled and burped, signaling that it had finished its job. I poured two cupsful, carried my cup to the sink, and gazed out of the kitchen window.

"Mom, come here! Look at the chicken yard!"

"What is it?" Mom asked, hurrying to stand beside me. "Why, it's Jethro! He's out in the chicken yard with the old settin' hen and look! Those baby chicks are climbing all over him."

I laughed. "And their mama doesn't mind a bit. He must have seen that she needed a little help with that big brood."

Mom shook her head. "Oh, Darcy! It's good to be home."

Chapter 45

Jethro was like any proud parent, loathe to leave his babies, but when I called, he finally meandered into the house. He had not eaten all the food in his dish, but I emptied it and filled it with fresh kibbles. His water dish was still full, but I emptied it too and refilled it at the sink.

Mom had gone upstairs to bathe and find more comfortable shoes. While she was gone, I cleaned up the blood spatters then scrubbed my hands until they were raw.

"I feel like a new woman, Darcy," Mom said, coming into the kitchen. Dressed in blue cotton slacks and a blue plaid blouse with her hair neatly combed, she looked as if she had stepped out of a fashion magazine.

"Well, look at you!" I said, grinning. "Are you, by chance, expecting a certain handsome lawyer to drop in?"

She winked and fluffed her hair. "One never knows. I'm ready to tackle that sewing machine, Darcy. It makes me heartsick to think it was ruined after lasting all these years, but I want to take a closer look and see if it might be repaired."

"Good idea," I agreed.

The lawn mower blade had broken through the top right side of the sewing machine cabinet, cleaving it and two drawers completely off. They lay on the floor by the dining table. The rest of the machine was intact.

Mom smiled and picked up one of the drawers.

"You know, I believe this can be fixed. It isn't splintered, just broken off from the rest of the machine. Oh, look, Darcy, here are some old spools of thread."

A small cotton pouch lay on the floor, evidently unseated from the drawer when it connected with the floor. From it spilled spools of red, yellow, and blue thread.

I squatted beside Mom and picked up the spool pouch.

"You're right. The thread may be rotten now, or perhaps it isn't; the colors are still bright. The drawers shouldn't be hard to put back and nail or glue in place. I wonder whose hands last used this thread, and how long ago?"

Mom shook her head. "No telling. This sewing machine was certainly well built. It must have been a family heirloom and Jeff intended to give it to his bride."

Picking up the drawer, she slid it back into its opening on the machine.

"Wait! What's wrong?" she asked. Frowning, she bent over to look inside the opening. "The drawer doesn't want to slide all the way in. I think something is stuck between it and the back of the machine."

"Pull the drawer out again," I said. "I'm going to feel behind it."

Reaching as far as I could into the recess, I touched something dry and crackly. Carefully, I lifted it between my thumb and forefinger and drew it from its dark hiding place. A small paper package tied with a blue ribbon lay in my palm.

Mom took it from my hand and turned it over. One word was scrawled across the paper in faded blue ink: "*Georgia.*"

Her hand holding the package shook.

"You open it, Darcy," she said. "I can't."

I slid the ribbon until it was free of the package. The old, yellowed paper was so dry it flaked off as I unfolded it.

A gold ring set with a brilliant, red ruby nestled in the paper.

For a moment, time turned backward. It was 1942 and a young soldier was going off to war. When he returned, he would offer his heart and his future to the young woman he loved. In the meantime, the ring would wait, a symbol of fresh hopes and dreams and two lives that would become one. But fate intervened. Dreams dissolved and hearts were broken and the ring lay hidden in the drawer, waiting for the day a young man would slip it on his young bride's finger. That day never came.

A mockingbird lit on the porch, imitating a trio of bird songs. Jethro nudged my hand and with one paw, poked the spools of thread. Mom and I gazed at the ring.

"I've never seen anything so beautiful," I whispered.

"It was to be Miss Georgia's," Mom murmured. "Jeff planned to give it to his sweetheart. To think that, all that time, he meant to marry her."

"Yes," I said. "He really loved her, Mom. Before he left for the war, he must have put this in here. Now we know. Jeff Thorne was a most honorable man. It's no wonder Miss Georgia loved him."

Chapter 46

"Do you know where Jeff Thorne is buried, Mr. Hopkins?" I asked.

The sound of Ranger barking accompanied Burke Hopkins's voice on the other end of the telephone conversation.

"I sure do, Darcy. After he died, I made it my business to know. Felt like it was my duty to sort of look after his grave site."

"Do you have time to take my mother and me to visit his grave? We'd both like to see where he was buried."

"You bet. How about tomorrow morning around nine o'clock?"

I grinned at Mom, who was anxiously listening to my end of the conversation. "Nine o'clock it is."

As I flicked off my cell phone, I felt happier than I had felt since that rainy night when Walter Harris appeared on our doorstop shortly before he was killed. It seemed that loose ends were being tied up, and maybe Mom and I could pass the rest of the summer gardening, and canning and freezing vegetables, and cutting herbs for drying.

I, of course, had my job at the newspaper if I wanted it. It might be fun to get paid for doing what I liked to do anyway, what I seemed to have a knack for falling into without even trying. Maybe now I would have time to put the finishing touches on the book I was writing. But, what better job than a newspaper reporter for sniffing out stories for a historical book?

I enjoyed spending time with Amy's twins. Maybe I should apply as a substitute teacher in the Ventris elementary school. Any of these jobs would keep me busy and perhaps keep me out of trouble.

Once again, I was grateful for Jake's foresight in buying the life insurance policy, and for the regular checks it provided. That substantial amount gave me the freedom to look at options for my life.

Finding the ruby ring after we returned home the previous day answered Mom's question about Jeff's intentions. With wood glue and a lot of patience, we got the old sewing machine back together, but what should we do with that beautiful ring? By rights, it was Miss Georgia's. But, if we gave it to her, she would certainly need to know the story behind it and if she knew, she would realize Jeff had died only a few miles away without ever trying to contact her.

The decision, however, was Mom's to make, not mine.

"Do you think you will ever tell Miss Georgia about the sewing machine and the ring?" I asked.

She gazed out the back door at the baby chicks running in the chicken yard and their mother, clucking them to her and scratching up worms. Jethro ambled over to the little family and stretched out in the sun, watching them.

"I don't know," Mom said softly. "I don't want to upset her. I remember that old saying Mama used to repeat, 'Least said, soonest mended.' I think that might apply here."

So, I left it at that.

About the Author

It may seem strange to some that a mild-mannered kindergarten teacher would become an author of cozy mysteries, but it's actually a good fit. A teacher is a word craft. So is a writer. A teacher wants the efforts of her labor to have a positive outcome. So does a writer. A teacher prays and hopes that each student has a positive take-away from her work. A writer hopes that for her readers too. A teacher would like each of the children in her classroom to achieve a satisfying life. Although she can't control that, as a writer she can control the way her books conclude!

A native Oklahoman, Blanche has a deep familiarity with the Sooner state, so it's the logical setting for her books. Her Cherokee heritage and feeling at home in the rural settings of Oklahoma are vividly woven into the background fabric of her books

We slid out of the truck, Mom carrying a bouquet of wild daisies, and followed Burke past several headstones to a recent grave site under a tall oak.

A bronze military marker confirmed this as the final resting place of Corporal Jefferson Thorne. I was not prepared for the wave of sorrow that engulfed me. The man who lay here had been my grandfather. He was a handsome man, a brave and caring man, a man who had made wrong decisions and paid the price for those decisions. Without him and many, many others with the same courage, I would not be enjoying the freedom I took so much for granted. He had lived through the horrors of war and endured hardships I would never know. With all my heart I wished I could have known Jeff Thorne, if for no other purpose than just to say, "Thanks."

I glanced at Mom. She smiled, although tears filled her eyes. Kneeling beside Jeff's grave, she placed the daisies.

We both saw the single red rose touching Jeff's headstone.

"It's good of you to bring a flower, Burke," Mom said, wiping her eyes.

Burke shook his head. "I didn't bring it. I never do. But every time I come, a red rose is right there where you see that one. So, you see, somebody besides us knows where Jeff lies."

I helped Mom to her feet. Holding hands, we bowed our heads and whispered the Lord's Prayer. Our visit finished, we turned to go. I felt a cool, soft breeze caress my face, although the wind was perfectly still.

"Goodbye, Jeff," I said. "I hope you found peace and love at last."

Chapter 48

Teaching! That was it. Surely, being a substitute teacher was a nice, sane, uneventful job which would open up fresh vistas and keep me out of trouble. Children were as bright and sparkling as new pennies. It would be fun to see them learn and I would enjoy getting re-acquainted with their parents. Many people I had known years ago were now parents and some early bloomers were even grandparents. Yes, it would be nice to substitute teach now and then and really become a part of my hometown once more.

I saw the relief in Mom's eyes when I mentioned my idea.

"Wonderful!" she said. "You don't get out enough, and I think you'd be a good teacher. It would be right up your alley and still give you time to write."

She didn't say so, but I suspected she thought teaching would be a nice job that did not include murderers wielding lawn mower blades or runaway teenagers or pretend pastors. It seemed a trip to Levi's Education Center was in order.

I stopped on my way out of the door.

"I keep thinking about the red rose on Jeff Thorne's grave. Who do you suppose left it?"

Mom pulled on her gardening gloves. "Perhaps someone at the nursing home where he lived was fond of him. Or . . ." She shook her head. "Or, maybe Miss Georgia found out he was buried there. He could have other relatives in Tahlequah, you know."

"Relatives! That would make them kin to us too. How would I find out? Maybe if I made a trip to that nursing home and talked to the people there…"

"Darcy!" Mom's voice was stern. "You are going to apply for a substitute teaching job, remember? It may be best to let well enough alone. If you delve into the life of my father, there's no telling what you will find. Think of Miss Georgia."

"You are right, Mom. Have a great morning among your herbs. See you later," I said and walked out the door to get in my Escape.

I drove with the window down, the wind fanning my face as I crossed the bridge over Lee Creek and headed toward town. The fragrance of herbs, wildflowers, and the elusive scent of the creek filled the car. It was great to be alive on such a morning!

Switching on the radio, I sang along. *"I warm my heart around a memory of days gone by and dreams that used to be."*

That song! I didn't want to warm my heart around memories any more. Memories were not enough. Memories were sad and they belonged to the past! However, I could not bring myself to switch off the radio. The song was so pretty! I was not sure if the words reminded me of Grant or Jake. I had memories of both, but Jake belonged in my past.

And Trace? What of Trace Hughes? It was funny—the flood made me realize how dear Grant was to me. Trace had been the one in danger of drowning, and I was grateful beyond measure that Mom and I reached him in time. But when I didn't know whether Tim Johnson had killed Grant or whether Grant had drowned, or what had happened, I realized that I did not want to ever lose him. Not a second time; it would have been too much. Would he ever ask me to marry him? Would I have the courage to say Yes? Being married to a lawman would not be easy.

The red rose kept clinging to my thoughts. Someone made that trip to Jeff's grave site often enough to leave a fresh flower; someone had cared about my grandfather. Did Burke know more than he told us? Did he know the name of the mysterious person?

Burke's memories of early-day Ventris County and his father would be an important part of the book I was writing. Maybe there was a long-ago story behind the red rose and Burke knew it. I hoped there would be time for a trip out to his farm before going back home.

Passing by the site of Old String's shack, I purposely looked the other way. I did not want to even glimpse the burned-out ruins. Hopefully, vines and grass would soon cover it and no one would know a house had been there. Maybe eventually we would forget that a man had been killed on the spot. But I feared I wouldn't forget and the image of Walter Harris would always be in my mind.

Glancing into the woods, I glimpsed a movement. Braking, I rolled down the passenger window and peered into the undergrowth. Something moved there, but what? A person? An animal?

Bushes moved again and I heard a rustling as something stirred in the shadows.

Could it be an injured animal? Maybe a car had hit a dog and it had crawled into the bushes. It might need help.

Opening the door, I eased around the car and bent to peer into the undergrowth. A tawny brown face with yellow eyes stared back at me. The animal growled and snarled. Underbrush crackled as it backed away and disappeared into the dense forest. Then all was quiet.

Heart pounding, I ran back around my car and jumped inside. I'd just had a close encounter with one of Ventris County's legends. The mountain lions were alive and well in these hills.

I started the car, rolled up all windows and sat there shivering. Was this the same big cat we had heard the night of the housewarming? Or were the woods full of them? Were the wild animals of Ventris County annoyed that our new house had encroached on their territory?

"Get hold of yourself, Darcy," I said aloud. "That was undoubtedly a cougar, but he ran! He was more afraid of you than you were of him."

Well, no. I didn't think he could have been more scared than I. Putting the car in gear, my tires squealed as I sped down the road toward Levi.

Rounding a blind curve, I stomped on the brake. A huge maple tree lay across the road, some of its quivering limbs brushing the hood of my car.

"What?" I gulped. Evidently it had just fallen. A few seconds sooner and I would have been under that tree, probably flattened by its weight. If I hadn't stopped for the cougar…

The continuous rains this summer caused many trees to lose their grip on the soggy ground. The slightest wind would send them down. This tree must have been another weather victim. And I would have been too, if I had passed along the road a few seconds earlier.

"Thank You, God," I whispered.

My hands shook so that it was hard to put the car into reverse. Slowly, I backed up until I found a place to turn around. The trip to Levi would have to wait. Would anybody believe my story about the panther that saved my life? Was his appearance at an opportune time merely a coincidence, or had the animal been a warning sent from the Lord? I remembered a preacher a long time ago saying that with God, there are no coincidences.

Feeling shaken and grateful, I drove back home. Everything happens for a reason, my mother had told me many times. Did that include what had just happened to me?

The July day seemed suddenly cold, and I could hardly wait to get my hands around a cup of Mom's hot coffee. She would believe my story about the panther, but I doubted that anyone else would. That encounter might be one of the things she and I kept to ourselves. The longer I lived, the more secrets I kept. Ventris County was placid only on the surface. Dark currents of mysteries, both natural and man-made, swirled in its depths. How many more were there that I had yet to discover?

Chapter 50

Light spilled from every window of the Jenkins home. It was early evening; the sun had dipped below the trees in the west, but darkness had not yet settled over the town. As Grant and I climbed the steep steps to the Jenkinses' front porch, I could not suppress a shudder at the memory of Mort lying at the bottom of those steps, the banister on the ground beside him.

"Darcy! Grant! Come join us," called Trace.

He sat in the shadows on the porch swing with his guitar; Melanie sat beside him.

I perched on the banister. Grant stood close, his hat in his hands.

"I can't thank you and Miss Flora enough," Trace said. "You saved my life. You found my little sister. I'll always be grateful. You are one of the bravest women I've ever known."

"It was an adventure," I said, glad that in the semi-darkness no one could see me blush. "How are you feeling, Melanie?"

"Wonderful! Miss Georgia and Miss Carolina are like family. They've made me feel so welcome!"

"Thank you too, Grant," Trace said. "Sorry to be so much trouble."

Grant looked down at the toe of his boot.

"Comes with the job," he muttered.

Miss Georgia stepped onto the porch and hugged both of us.

"It's about time you showed up," she said. "Flora and Jackson got here twenty minutes ago."

Her face was wreathed in smiles and she had a lilt to her voice. How would she feel if she knew about the visit Mom and I had made to a lonely grave site? What would she say if she saw the ruby ring?

Grasping my hand, she said, "Come on inside, all of you. I think everyone is here now. Carolina and I have an announcement to make."

As we stepped into the living room, the hum of several conversations met us. Miss Carolina appeared carrying a tray of cookies. The fragrance of coffee wafted in from the kitchen.

Pat looked up from the old picture album she and Burke Hopkins had been thumbing through and waved at us.

"Come sit by us, you two," Mom called. She patted the cushion of the sofa where she and Jackson sat.

"What is this big announcement?" I whispered to Mom.

She shook her head. "I don't have any idea."

Miss Carolina set her tray on the coffee table and walked to the fireplace to stand beside Miss Georgia.

"Welcome, one and all," she said. "This gathering reminds me of other times, when Georgia and I were young. This old house knew some parties then, I can tell you. Those were good years!"

Smothering a grin, I thought about those long-ago get-togethers. I had a vision of sedate play parties and taffy pulls. The grim old judge probably had a long list of things he would not allow.

As if she read my thoughts, Miss Georgia said, "I'll admit that most of our parties happened when Papa was out of town. He was a circuit judge, you know, and did a lot of traveling."

"Wait!" Trace said. "Someone is on the porch."

With two quick steps, he opened the screen door. Jasper stepped inside, his eyes wide and scared as he glanced around the crowded living room.

"My hero!" called Melanie. "Come and sit beside Miss Kitty and me, Jasper."

His face turned red to the roots of his hair.

"No, I reckon I'm all right where I am," he mumbled and remained standing beside the door as if he might bolt into the night at any moment.

Miss Carolina smiled at him and continued.

"We've talked over this matter with Trace and Melanie. Sister and I have been rattling around in this big old house for a good many years and it's time we put a stop to it. We've asked Melanie to stay with us, and she and her brother have consented. She'll have her own room upstairs and when the baby comes, he'll have his own little nursery."

Miss Georgia smiled, two spots of color in her cheeks. "I'm so excited I don't think I can wait. In fact, we're going to start fixing up that nursery tomorrow." She paused and smiled at Mom. "I feel like maybe the Lord has given me a second chance with this little baby."

My mouth dropped open. I stared at the Jenkins twins then glanced at Mom. She looked as startled as I felt. What a novel idea! And, why not? In fact, I could see the reasoning behind it. How nice it would be to have Melanie close by. I wanted to get better acquainted with her, and surely I could help with the baby.

Spontaneously, we all started to clap and offer congratulations.

"Wait, wait! Before we go any further, I want to say something," Trace said.

Getting up from his chair, he strode to the fireplace and stood beside Miss Georgia and Miss Carolina, facing us.

"I want to apologize to you all. I'm going to church Sunday and apologize to the whole congregation. In effect, I lied to you. I passed myself off as my father, a preacher. I ask you all to forgive me."

"Of course you're forgiven," called Jackson. "You may not be ordained, but anybody who can liven up our congregation like you did deserves to be forgiven. I kind of like clapping my hands in time to the music. I hope you'll stay."

Trace shook his head. "No, I can't stay. My sister will be well taken care of. She loves these two women, Miss Georgia and Miss Carolina and, as a matter of fact, so do I. I love you all."

He glanced at me as he spoke. Returning his smile, I felt a welcome warmth. Trace was a dear person, a friend, but that's all he would ever be. He was not, nor would he ever be, Jake. I did not feel devastated that he would be leaving. He would never be happy in a small town like Levi.

Grant re-crossed his legs and cleared his throat.

"You'll find another pastor," Trace said, "an honest one, this time, and I'll go back to Atlanta and do what I like to do best, continue with my music. 'Thank you' seems very weak, but thanks, all of you, for accepting me without question. Levi, Oklahoma, will always be special to me."

In between hugs and handshakes and a general happy hubbub, Grant's phone rang.

He listened for a moment and said, "I'll be there, Jim."

Turning to me, he said, "Sorry, Darcy," then planted a kiss on my cheek and moved toward the door.

Mom sighed. "The life of a lawman."

I nodded. "He will never change."

~ The End ~

About the Author

It may seem strange to some that a mild-mannered kindergarten teacher would become an author of cozy mysteries, but it's actually a good fit. A teacher is a word craft. So is a writer. A teacher wants the efforts of her labor to have a positive outcome. So does a writer. A teacher prays and hopes that each student has a positive take-away from her work. A writer hopes that for her readers too. A teacher would like each of the children in her classroom to achieve a satisfying life. Although she can't control that, as a writer she can control the way her books conclude!

A native Oklahoman, Blanche has a deep familiarity with the Sooner state, so it's the logical setting for her books. Her Cherokee heritage and feeling at home in the rural settings of Oklahoma are vividly woven into the background fabric of her books.

MORE GREAT BOOKS BY BLANCHE!

THE DARCY & FLORA COZY MYSTERY SERIES, BOOKS 1-4

Goshen Cemetery lay quiet and peaceful under a benevolent spring sky. Darcy Campbell and her mother, Flora Tucker, had no inkling that in a few moments, the scene would change and they would face a horror on the ground and a threat from above, beyond their imaginations.

Becoming entangled in a centuries-old legend, being targeted by a group of ruthless men, and discovering a long-lost love were not in Darcy's plans when she returned to her birth place, Levi, Oklahoma. She merely wanted to soak up the peace of her mother's home and try to heal the wounds left from her husband's death. Fate, however, had other plans for Darcy and Flora.

READ A FREE CHAPTER OR GET YOUR COPY TODAY!
At www.Pen-L.com/TheCemeteryClub.html

Before the long nightmare ended, Darcy would often wish her mother had not opened that letter from an unknown woman. But, she did open it and shared it with her daughter, plunging both Darcy Campbell and Flora Tucker into a tale of an unsolved mystery, a web of secrets, and the discovery of an unsuspected traitor.

In tracking down clues about the disappearance of a young woman, Darcy and Flora leave their hometown of Levi, Oklahoma, and drive to Amarillo, Texas, then back again. Following leads that have long been covered, both women find more than one surprise including some discoveries about themselves.

Read a Free chapter or get your copy today!
At www.Pen-L.com/GraveShift.html

Darcy Campbell might have expected life in a small Oklahoma town nestled in the beautiful Ozark foothills to be as idyllic as the scenery. That, however, is not what she finds when she returns to her hometown of Levi after the death of her husband.

One autumn morning, Darcy and her mother, Flora Tucker, are enjoying a cup of coffee in their hundred-year old farmhouse when Darcy gets an urgent telephone call. The contractor who is digging the foundation for their new home insists that Darcy drop everything and come to the building site as quickly as she can. He has found a mysterious object deep in a hand-dug well and he needs Darcy's help in retrieving it.

The ancient, crumbling package pulled from the well contains two items that are as shocking as they are inscrutable. In trying to decipher the meaning of these long-buried objects, Darcy and Flora discover a dark secret from their family's past.

A kidnapping, a brush with death, and a stranger's greed add to the mix. The era of World War I becomes enmeshed with the present day as Darcy and Flora unravel a tangled web of deceit that has ensnared their family.

Read a Free chapter or get your copy today!
At www.Pen-L.com/BestLeftBuried.html

Don't miss
THE NED MCNEIL MYSTERY SERIES
Cozy mysteries with an extra shiver!!

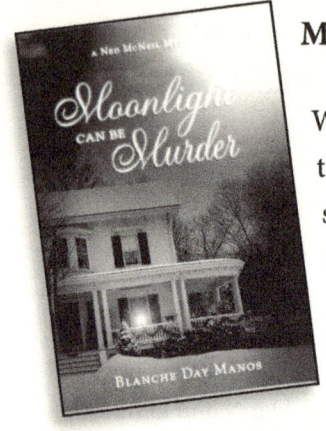

MOONLIGHT CAN BE MURDER

When widow Nettie "Ned" McNeil returns to her hometown of Ednalee, Oklahoma, she finds her uncle lying in a pool of blood. Obsessed, she risks her own life pursuing the killer who will stop at nothing to hide a deadly secret.

**Read a FREE chapter
or get your copy today at
WWW.PEN-L.COM/MoonlightCanBeMurder.html**

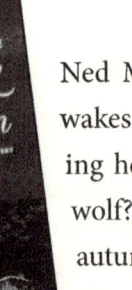

BY THE FRIGHT OF THE SILVERY MOON

Ned McNeil is haunted by a nightmare that wakes her in the middle of the night, leaving her gasping for breath. A dog—or is it a wolf?—howling in her yard under the brilliant autumn moon sends chills down her spine. Get ready for a page turner; a cozy mystery with an extra shiver that just may keep you up at night, even when the moon isn't full!

**Read a FREE chapter or get your copy today at
WWW.PEN-L.COM/ByTheFrightOfTheSilveryMoon.html**

Moonstruck and Murderous

A cold wind can send shivers down your spine!

The month is March—a strange month, noted for its fickle weather—but this March has an added strangeness in the form of two full moons. Could they be the reason for murder to strike the small town of Ednalee, Oklahoma? Some think so. In the quiet little town, who could be to blame?

But there is more than one suspect, and before the month ends, the murderer strikes again and yet again.

Could the slayings involve the Carver Mansion? Mystery surrounds the estate. Does the ancient house attract evil?

Perhaps the bloodthirsty predator who stalks these historic grounds is affected by the blue moon? Amateur sleuth Ned McNeil must find out before even more people die.

Is the killer moonstruck or murderous—or both?

Get your ebook or print copy today at
WWW.PEN-L.COM/MOONSTRUCKANDMURDEROUS.HTML

Dear Reader,
If you enjoyed this book enough to review it for Goodreads, B&N, or Amazon.com, I'd appreciate it!
Thanks, Blanche

Find more great reads at
Pen-L.com

Made in the USA
Coppell, TX
02 September 2023